STORIES OF A CAMPUS

A COLLECTION OF SHORT STORIES

STORIES OF A CAMPUS
A COLLECTION OF SHORT STORIES

MALLIKARJUN PATIL

ATLANTIC PUBLISHERS AND DISTRIBUTORS

Published by
ATLANTIC PUBLISHERS AND DISTRIBUTORS
B-2, Vishal Enclave, New Delhi-110 027
Phones : 541 3460, 542 9987

Sales Office
4215/1, Ansari Road, Darya Ganj, New Delhi-110 002
Phones : 327 3880, 328 5873, 328 0451
Fax : 91-11-328 5873
e-mail : info@atlanticbooks.com
web : www.atlanticbooks.com

ISBN 81-7156-948-X

Typeset at
APD Computer Graphics, Delhi

Printed in India at
Nice Printing Press, Delhi

DEDICATED TO

DR. NANDA M. PATIL
THE DEAREST OF MINE

PREFACE

I am happy to publish a collection of short stories entitled *Stories Of A Campus*. This book contains ten stories written in my own technique and style. For evidence the story 'My Encounter with a Spirit' is written in a mode of language that is akin to Raja Rao's as reflected in his *Kanthapura*. Be it known to my readers that most of the characters and situations depicted here are fictitious and no objection can be made against their identification with anyone.

In this regard, a word or two must be said about Pampapati University about which much is written in these tales. Pampapati University is a fictitious name and no institution of that name exists anywhere. The situations of this Campus are merely the children of their author's imagination.

I hope it is a right time to tell about those who influenced me to indulge in the art of story-telling. I am proud to say that great writers like Charles Dickens, Thomas Hardy and D.H. Lawrence have made their own impact upon me. Particularly I have to acknowledge Hardy's influence in shaping my creative sensibility.

Presently it is my bounden duty to thank those who inspired me in bringing out this book of stories which is the original part of my creative thinking. First of all, I am grateful to Prof. M. Muniyamma, the Vice-Chancellor of Gulbarga University, Gulbarga. Equally I am thankful to Professors P.N. Rao, Revd. S.S. Gokavi, C.Y. Yeravintelimath, Chandrashekhar Patil, Giraddi Govindraj, Sarojini Shintri, A.A. Mutalik Desai, V.C. Chavadi, S.P. Hiremath and V.R. Kulli who encouraged me in my creative enterprises. Also I am thankful to M/s Atlantic Publishers and Distributors New Delhi for their neat publication of this work.

Finally, I am indebted to my *artiste*-wife Dr. Nanda M. Patil whose encouragement helped me in bringing out this book.

MALLIKARJUN PATIL

CONTENTS

1

MONEY MAKING BUSINESS

'GOOD MORNING sir,' Geeta said to Prof. Ramrao at 10 o'clock morning.

'Oh! Good Morning. How're you?' In turn, Ramrao greeted Geeta smiling upon her. Meanwhile Suresh, his another student wished him good morning rather undecidedly and desired to see him. Understanding his niggardliness, Ramrao asked him to see him some other time later. He was not interested in him as he had not worked for his welfare. The Professor knew that the boy Suresh also helped those whom he did not like. Ramrao helped only those who either bribed him or served him with loyalty. He was a man of worldliness — very shrewd and practical. A perfect cynic, he saw everyone with doubt. A worldly — worldly-wise. Only when he realised that a particular person was really good, he would entertain him, otherwise he would not even spit upon. Not to speak of Ramrao had no friends as such. As he did not believe in values, he hesitated in befriending people. Nor did he entertain any laity. But his contacts with the writers and rich were vast and he enjoyed a countrywide reputation. He was a columnist. Because of this, many people had known him. However, this was not to enjoy the fruit of friendship but only to see that Ramrao would write about them.

After Geeta, the beauty queen, had gone into her research room, Ramrao called in his peon. The servant was given some money to bring tea. When the Professor was about to close his door, one Dr. Reddy from a North Indian University arrived there. The purpose of his visit was obviously to strike out a deal

'Good Morning Professor.'

'Oh! Very Good Morning Reddy. Come in. How're you?'

'I'm fine. How're you sir?'

'Nice as the bills're coming.'

'Oh!...Bills...Which bills?' Reddy asked enquiringly.

'The evaluation fees of 1999. Have you forgotten it? I think you're not worried about your financial matters,' Ramrao finished his say in his casual voice even without giving the other any chance to poke his nose.

'That's true. How much have you received?'

'Just five thousand rupees,' the elder replied passively. As the amount was small, it did not attract him.

'So you're happy today,' the younger burst grinning.

'Naturally. What matters us these days is money, isn't it? If you don't have money, nobody will talk to you. Even God won't bless you. No money; no meaning. Now money is the god of earth..... Yea, it's all. Ramrao added the last as an afterthought.

'Oh!.... Don't you think man's more important than money?' the other put it decidedly.

'My goodness!....Who cares for man these days?' Ending it abruptly, Ramrao lit a Charminar cigar and closed the door smoothly. He was happy, for Reddy had come there to talk to him about a Ph.D. *viva-voce*. Reddy's student's dissertation had come to Ramrao for an evaluation. Since Ramrao had found it below the mark, just to exploit the other, he had not yet returned it. As it was guided by Reddy, he withheld it for sometime hoping that Reddy would see him personally. Therefore, there was Reddy today.

'Let's come to the point', the guest began.

'Ph.D. assessment?' Ramrao shook his head.

'Yes'.

'The work falls below the line. I don't know why it's not properly planned and written. There're many mistakes and the presentation is incoherent', obviously Ramrao stopped for a breathforce.

'D'you think doctorate degrees can be given to such dissertations?' he added waiting for an eager reply.

'Yes, there're mistakes. I know it. B... but...'Reddy stammered as Ramrao's tone changed soon.

'In thirty years of my service, I didn't receive such a third-rate thesis for an evaluation', told Ramrao in a huff.

'Yes, it's true. I know the work isn't superb. That's why I'm meeting you in person. As Russian is a second language to our students, we can't blame them too. But it doesn't mean that they mustn't master it and make their research sincerely. Anyway let it be there. Now tell me how much...?' Reddy begged the other for a favour.

'You know my demands very well,' Ramrao returned a smile to the other's chagrin.

'Sir it's a poor student's case. Therefore, now I'm here,' implored the other for a personal benefit.

'I don't care a poor or rich case. If at all you want a good remark, meet my demands lest your student won't get a degree', Ramrao said it as though he had been a hard-hearted criminal. Then he smiled and with his smile he said 'Five', a single word as a cure to this. Then pleading on Reddy's side and stubbornness on Ramrao's, went on for more than half an hour. Ramrao was an intellectual — far more corrupt. Everyone knew his intellectual arrogance. Although people respected him, he was not a profound scholar — only a mediocre genius. His academic achievement was not sparkled with brilliance. He would not prepare for classes. Nor would he take them regularly. Anyway he did not care for his duty — good or evil. He knew he would get his salary anyhow. What mattered him most was only moneymaking business. He was a Professor and for many times he had been the chairman of his department and a member of Senate, Syndicate and Academic Council of Pampapati University. Even as a Professor of Russian, he had been to Mascow, London, New

York and other capitals of European countries. As he was a Ph.D. guide, he saved no efforts to make money. Money was for him everything — his joy and woe. Even a whore. As he enjoyed a countrywide fame, he was often on the panel of BOS, BOE, BOA and interviews. He evaluated KAS, IAS and other 'S' papers. His interests lay in getting links, befriending key figures and in collecting cheques. Even he did not care for small remuneration. His fees were in terms of thousands. Sometimes for the sake of money, Ramrao did whatever he could.

Ramrao was a trickster — a wise chap. None was more cold and calculative than he in the whole campus. He never helped people with information. He was reserved too. He did not speak more than necessary and his words were often ambiguous. An ordinary person could not understand him easily. Instead Ramrao knew how to elicit information from those who came to him. Nor did he give any advice to people whenever they sought him for it. In fact, he did not care for others. Whenever people or students sought him for suggestions, he asked them for something. Those who gave him this *something* would get his assistance at once, while those who did not, or delayed it, were made to meet him at a time when he was out of station. Those who got help from him gave him a fixed amount. His trickery and selfishness were compelling. He employed lies soundly. His pretensions looked truthful too. His words were very fine — rather mesmerising. Almost like honey. No wonder, he was known for niceties. He consoled those who were angry against him and crushed those who rebelled. It is because of his crookedness, he was surnamed Mr Cunningham.

At last the business was fixed at three thousand rupees and Dr. Reddy left the campus happy.

Ramrao loved money beyond everything. He devised every way he could to amass it. He exploited all — the rich and poor, students and scholars and those in service. Besides his duty as usual, he gave talks, delivered lectures and wrote columns just for the sake of wealth. Money was his credo. What not? He received valuable gifts from students and others alike. One of his students presented him a scooter, a research scholar gave him cupboards and a businessman helped him in getting his house constructed. These are only samples. He received gifts in any possible manner during a period of three decades of his service. In fact, he exploited all those who came in his circle. Therefore, those who trusted him suffered.

Ramrao flourished like a businessman. Happy was he always. Even he did not know how much money he had earned. As he accumulated it from whomsoever he could, he deposited it in many banks as he was afraid of tax people. Sometimes he forgot certain accounts too. But his wife was there to remind him of such things. No wonder, he enjoyed Kubera's rank in light terms.

In spite of all this, Ramrao was not happy. He was all the way restless. His passion for money had made him tense. With his wealth, went his misfortunes. Can a man who is always after money be happy or peaceful? His worries and anxieties were there as ever before. After all, these were the very problems he had really invited.

Ramrao kept his people at bay. He never entertained anyone intimately. He was a man who could command their respect on account of his seniority, connections, discipline and niceties. When once some students misbehaved in his class to warn them he burst out:

'D'you know that your behaviour is counted here? If you behave and study well, you thrive well, otherwise', he said them, 'your fate will be permanently sealed.' He continued his ethic without expecting a yes or no from students who, in curiosity, sat silent gaping at him earnestly. They were despair-struck. Some students specially ladies were eager to know the standard of behaviour imposed in University. Though University is a seat of higher education, a sensitive girl thought 'things forbidden took place there.'

'In this regard, I'd like to tell you a story,' Ramrao began slyly. 'See a University, or for that matter any other higher institution of power is like a knife and the learners like you are an apple. If apple falls on knife who will be ruined?'

'Apple sir', said some boys and girls anxiety-stricken.

'Then if the knife falls on apple who'll be destroyed?' Ramrao's second question was equally stunning.

'Again the apple will be destroyed', students replied it together. There was a wave of dejection sweeping over them.

So reading the students' heart and secretly smiling at them like a sage Ramrao tried to sum up his hypothesis.

'In both cases only the apple is ruined. So behave and study cautiously.' There was every sign of wisdom in Ramrao's advice. His words were full of practical experience.

There were six students doing their Ph.D. under Ramrao's guidance. One of them understanding his mode of guidance stopped his studies; the second worked for some time but because of difference of opinion, left him; while the third, a lady did a fair amount of progress but she discontinued her study as she could not meet his demands. However she was a bright student, her fate was sealed, for she was not ready to pay him.

The remaining three — a lady and two boys — adjusted to his den of villainy. One of the two boys under Ramrao's guidance possessed all niceties which the other had expected. He was one Mr Huchchappa. In fact, knowing his guide's nature better than all others, he gave him bags of grains, fruits and vegetables occasionally. Even in his hours of need, he helped him financially. Upto the time he secured his degree, he had paid the Professor not less than Rs. 25,000 both in cash and kind. That was why Ramrao was kind to him. Likewise on getting his degree, Huchchappa presented him a refrigerator which Mrs. Ramrao was greatly in need of.

The other boy who was doing his Ph.D. under Ramrao was also good. But the greatest mistake his guide found in him was his honesty. He worked well and he did not like to oil his hand. Therefore, the boy was not destined to take a degree there.

Then there was the case of a fair lady as well. She was very pretty. Her beauty had carried away Mr. Ramrao. She looked as if she had inherited the beauty and grace of Damayanti, the dark-eyed maid of Indian myths. Upon this faultless and slender-waisted maiden there waited countless men at least to have a glance at her. Never among the students of Pampapati University, such a mortal maid came to study there before. She was dark-eyed but was fairer than the legendary dame. Red as coral were her lips; her teeth shone like jasmine. Her eyes were like lotus blooms and her face was always enticing. Her angelic beauty attracted one and all. People compared her to every Miss Universe they had seen and heard. In their view, she was more beautiful than Helen, Sita, whom not even Diana. Ramrao was happy to compare her to Manroe. Just the same, many people stood on the way for a while just to see her beauty. Even they saw her with an eye of love. Her supreme beauty, shapely limbs, dark eyes, rare facial radiance, slender-waist and rich attire had made her a perfect bride. Those who could not have a glance at her or could not talk to her called her a witch; and those who had been familiar to her really talked of her in superlative terms.

Even Prof. Ramrao, though middle-aged and utterly money-minded, took her his Ph.D. student only with an eye of love. He was fifty while his dream girl had been just twenty-five. What a wonder? What a difference? A difference of twenty-five years persisted between them. He too knew he was double of her age. But he thought that 'everything was fair in love and war.' As she was interested in Russian, she too loved him best for his knowledge. Although he was the most corrupt teacher and enjoyed notoriety, he did not ask her for any penny. Her beauty alone had made him over-joyed.

One day when Ramrao sat alone, Geeta came to him greeting. After the 'good mornings', the discussion between them began.

'Anton Tchekow is certainly a great writer,' she told him, while his eyes were cast on her. Admittedly he would smile upon her before he could begin.

'Yes; he's certainly a great writer', replied he moving his hand.

'In what way should I bring in a comparison between Tchekov and Premchand?' Geeta would ask him returning a smile.

Already the acquaintance between them had grown up into courtship. But it was Ramrao who had alone developed it into a sort of love. As she was innocent, she simply tolerated him. She had thought that he was a great man. So she never worried of this, though most of the times, her pent up emotions made her to succumb to his instinctual desires.

One day Ramrao sure of his colleagues' absence, closed the door as usual. Beside her, he was seeing her draft. He had sat close touching her now and then. When his desire was not quenched and he did not find Geeta rather blushing, he would kiss her heavenly areas. Surprising enough, the lady tolerated it with divine patience. Meanwhile if at all she returned him smiles, she did it only out of her respect. And her falling in his arms was not an exception to this.

Great is the power of beauty. Her angelic presence, her bewitching look and appreciation she received for it, made Ramrao almost fall in love with her. Even without consulting his wife who had already borne him three sons, or caring for Geeta's approval, Ramrao decided to marry her.

Days passed thus lingeringly.

One day Geeta took her degree and when she met her guide, the latter burst :

'We've to meet again.'

'Okay,' said she smiling.

On deciding to meet each other on the next Monday, both sipped tea and left for home. Ramrao was sure that he would marry her as many times she had nodded for that. What a wonder? He also briefed it to his wife to wash out her shock and bewilderment. Likewise, he had made an alternative arrangement for his second wife.

Ramrao did not know his fate had already been decided in heaven. On the appointed time, even ten minutes earlier, he went to the place for awaiting her. Ramrao waited. Ten minutes passed. Another ten minutes passed. Even an hour went by. He waited and waited. This waiting for a love recollected him Hardy's poem 'A Broken Appointment.' He did it all as he did not know that there was a slip between a cup and lip.

An unhappy Ramrao went home cursing his fate. Though he tried to sleep he could not. Today he was totally shaken by love sickness. To add fuel to the fire no sooner he tried to sleep at the stroke of midnight, than a paralysis struck him.

OOO

2

PEDDANNA'S ECCENTRICITY

'DON'T MISTAKE me sir,' Pedda(anna) requested Bhimanna, a Deputy Registrar(DR), Pampapati University.

'Alright Pedda,' replied the other smiling.

'Many people mistake me sir,' Pedda spoke to his boss.

'Yes, gap of communication leads to that,' said Bhimanna, a well-bodied officer. He was good for good. His lip word was 'tit for tat.' Since Pedda was a humorous person, he had allowed him some freedom in the office.

'Why misunderstanding takes place sir?' Pedda burst again as if he did not understand the other's earlier explanation.

'Didn't I tell you that gap of understanding leads to it? Also know that misunderstanding leads to misunderstanding,' Bhimanna spoke a little angrily which Pedda could not comprehend. Consequently seeing Bhimanna crimson red, Pedda trotted to his table.

A short while later, when Pedda took a file to Bhimanna, the latter noticed some crucial mistakes done in it.

'Pedda, why you've made many mistakes here,' asked the DR a little angrily.

'Somehow it's done. Kindly don't mistake me sir,' prompt was Pedda's plea.

'Mistake?...Who's mistaking you?'

'Just I said sir,' Pedda finished his say.

Thus, the day in a bustle of work wore out. However all the

clerks went off home, Pedda remained in the office for some time and seizing an opportunity, he came to his boss.

'Please don't mistake me for that sir,'burst he there.

'Alright', spoke the other smiling.

One day a repulsive incident took place in a bachelors quarters of the Pampapati University. When in a morning, Narasamma was at her home alone, Pedda went there. Meanwhile the dame had gone to take a bath, while Pedda relaxed outside reading a newspaper. He sat there waiting for her husband Narayan. But the crawling of a snake in the bathroom forced the woman to rush out naked into the hall where Pedda, the eccentric was sitting. No wonder, the woman at once afraid of the snake, mistaking the man for her husband embraced him suddenly. But soon she came to know that it was Pedda and she thought that dying by snakebite was better than this. Now she stood frozened. For a while, Pedda too closed the door, through which a person was watching. This awkward position petrified both Pedda and Narasamma.

'Why you...you came here nonsense?' she cried soon. Then putting her hands to her being, she rushed into the kitchen. Barebodied she was. Not a single cloth adored her golden flesh. Her breast shone. She looked big and bright. Awfully Pedda was happy to have seen her, embraced and felt her. He knew she was none other than his wife's sister. As so both the families had been close to each other. This is how today he had come there but then his cousin had gone to a grocery. Nor did the woman close the door inside. To add fuel to the fire the snake had come therein. However, nothing intentionally had taken place. But still the danger was lurking as Pedda was, instead of going away, trying to beg her pardon, while Narasamma was still in a state of haze as her dress were in the room where Pedda relaxed.

No sooner Pedda was to approach her for an excuse than her husband burst in.

'Oh! How're you?' Narayan asked Pedda curiously, while Pedda welcomed the other as if the house was his.

'O!... an event sir...'Pedda said something woefully.

'Wh...What's happened?'

'A snake...A snake crawled in your house, while your wife was bathing. The maid rushed out into the hall and at once she embraced me sir...'

Now Pedda himself was on the verge of sobbing. Nor was Narayan happy. The depth of his sorrow was too much. He was close to tears. So was his wife inside. People knew Narayan was very gentle. He had never harmed people in the vicinity. But on this day he did not know why god was rather cruel to allow this event to take place there.

'Why you came here in my absence?' he spoke angrily.

'Just to give your money sir.' Pedda to save his soul returned the other his Rs. 500 which he had really wished to give him later.

'All right; don't tell it to anyone. It's a question of my family prestige. Understand it?' Narayan briefed the other over the need of keeping the event undisclosed.

'Anyway, I didn't come here with an evil intention sir. Only I came here to pay you the balance. And who knew that that bloody snake would appear in your house. She's anyway my wife's sister. I too am a pure person as well. So you need not scold her,' Pedda went on endlessly before he went off. But the dismayed Narayan was not yet happy as he had anticipated the inglorious repercussion of the morning cataclysm.

'Where did you go?' Asked Narasamma her husband.

'Where else... but to the shop...' he replied guilt conscious.

Sad was he still emitting long breaths of displeasure.

'Why didn't you latch the door outside?' she asked him. She was right. Had he bolted the door outside, nobody would enter the house during the time of her bath. This made him more guilty.

Now he did nothing but expressed his sorrow.

There was a deadly silence.

'Why did you embrace that dirty fellow?' asked he gathering his all courage.

'No; when the snake entered the bathroom, I hurried for my life. As I knew none came to our house at this time of the day and as I knew always it was you who sat here reading, I embraced the figure just because of the fear,'said she.

This description was vivid enough for Narayan even to die. The word 'embrace' shocked him to the core. As he disliked people seeing his beautiful wife with an evil eye, he did not even go to anybody's house in the neighbourhood. People knew Narayan's wife was a fair looking dame. Even the clerical group held the view that Narasamma was the most beautiful woman in the campus. With their appreciation also went their jealousy. They disliked the match. They thought Narayan was not handsome enough to her beauty. But she had never complained over this. Nor he either. In fact, they were the happy couple made for each other. Unable to bear this, some evil-eyed and bestial people giggled at him. Nothing was more tragic to them than some men's effort to separate them through the agency of a whore. Once there was an effort to rape her. So on realising the disgust of this, they had come to the University quarters from the city. However the problems of these small houses had been not inconsiderable. These houses were small and for a stranger they looked like a hostel. The quarters were nucleated too. Besides, extra-marital relationships were seen there at times. Recently Chandru had caught his wife Radha, an SDC red-handed, when she was seen with Venkappa flirting. In another incident, an FDC Hanumappa had tried to rape his friend's wife as he had lost his, long ago. This is how some people had maintained extra-marital connections. Even many people had a confusion in tracing their houses as everyone looked alike without numbers. Usually the low class people, greedy clerks and crooked officers were in search of golden deers. Entering the houses without permission was not uncommon. In fact, the whole building looked like a den of villainy — all in wilderness. This kind of things would have not been seen elsewhere.

Narayan who sat still for minutes got up then only because of his wife's long persuasion.

'I'm very sorry,' said she lowering her head.

'I don't complain you my dear. I'm afraid of Pedda's gossip,' he spoke dryly.

'Don't worry, we'll take a promise from him,' Narasamma consoled her beset husband. But none was worried of the snake which had been, of course, the reason *de etra* of all this unhappiness. But it had already gone as well. Now somehow Narasamma made her husband ready for the office.

No sooner Narayan had come to the office than many of his colleagues began smelling the event. Unfortunately Pedda had spread it as he could not maintain secrecy. He first disclosed even his wife's affair with a neighbour, a decade ago. This day he did it rather timidly but it had reached almost many. Upset Narayan could not help facing many an awkward encounter. So when he met Bhimanna the other smiled at him.

'What's wrong with you today?'

'Nothing sir... a snake'd got into our house...'

Bhimanna was, however good enough not to enter into other's affairs.

Hardly not much later friends began asking Narayan whether there had been any truth in what Pedda spoke of things. Somehow Narayan would dodge them. Soon he was safe upon his chair. Yet now and then fellow workers would look at him or jeer. Although Pedda worked in the same office, then he was not seen there. Mostly he had been on leave. But what a wonder! The news had become an open secret. When he had been alone Narayan meditated over this mystery. In confusion even he talked to himself. The mock gestures thrown at him had shaken his nerves. But soon Pedda's arrival there silenced Narayan's monologue.

'O! ...You've already spread your filth here?' burst Narayan angry.

'No brother, I didn't do it. It's done by Gopalayya,' Pedda tried to save his skin. He looked like a devil that had come there after having destroyed everything noble.

'I'm sorry Narayan. Please don't mistake me,' Pedda went on imploring, though Narayan had not yet started his drilling.

'Get out rascal,' like a bomb Narayan exploded. Ferocious he looked. This made Pedda run away, while some people in the office overheard the hitch.

What a nonsense? Again at the end of the day, Pedda came to his cousin for tendering his apology.

This made Narayan pounce upon him as he ran to Bhimanna. The latter was surprised over the hustle and enquired them.

'He's mistaken me sir,' said Pedda first.

'What's the matter, tell me?' Bhimanna asked them. No doubt, he had not yet known their entire story.

'Sir yesterday I went to see Narayan who had been to a shop. I waited for him awhile. Unfortunately, his wife afraid of a snake while bathing rushed out in horror and she embraced me...'

This forced Narayan to beat the fellow. So he hit him heavily to wounds. Truly had there Bhimanna not been, Narayan would dispatch Pedda straight to hell.

Soon the situation was made normal.

The aged people died, while the young became old but Pedda did not stop his harping over the matter though everyone had forgotten the event fairly. Whenever someone sat beside him to pass his time, Pedda would disclose everything. Equally those who wanted to insult Narayan would use this man to their advantage. One day when Narayan was in the market, Pedda opened the chapter and insulted him again.

This pained Narayan like anything turning him nauseating.

Subsequently Mrs. and Mr. Narayan came to a conclusion that they could not live in the campus. Pedda's revival of the old wounds continued to grieve them. So realising the futility of their further stay there, they decided to take a transfer to Onur, a PG Centre of the same University. They also prayed Pampapati, the God of the town, while Mr. Narayan requested the Vice-Chancellor for a transfer. No doubt, the next week, when the eccentric Pedda wished to see them again to tender his grand apology, the latter had disappeared.

ooo

3

KALLAPPA'S SEARCH FOR A BRIDE

AS TO everyone love for Kallappa was a thing of eternal fascination and he wanted to marry as soon as he would select a bride. Since his sister got married to a brickie years ago and as his mother had been aged now, his friends and relatives advised him to raise a family. His father had died years ago and Kallappa had been made a responsible person in the family. Besides, how could his aged mother live alone at home either? Even he was aged thirty and he had a good job to support his future. Under these circumstances, Lakkappa was right in persuading Kallappa to start for searching a bride.

Well on the appointed day, Lakkappa came to Kallappa's house in full gaiety. By then Lakkappa too was ready. And immediately they both started to think about their journey

'Aunt today we're going to find you a daughter-in-law,' Lakkappa told the old woman, who after her breakfast, had rested in a hall.

'Thank God...I'm happy today,' said the old woman looking in the sky.

'You'd be happy always,' the other returned her a broad smile.

'How can I be happy without a full house?' The oldmaid put it jovially. She was right. Though aged thirty her son had not yet thought of marrying.

'Ok! Lakku I bless both of you... Return home soon and

successful…Today I've prayed to goddess Ellamma to bless us,' said she heartily.

Boramma, the old woman, for that was her name also added that she had assured the deity some sacrifice in case she got a good bride who can live with her happily. Boramma was very traditional. Her sense of religiosity was not yet weakened. She was a devoted wife in the days bygone; presently she was a benign mother; and in the days to come, she wanted to become a good mother-in-law. 'But who knows,' she would think, 'what kind of daughter-in-law Ellamma would bestow her?'

'Right…We'll go mother,' her son told her expecting her blessings.

'Alright my son. I wish you all the best heaven can give you,' said she happily turning to see them departing. Soon with a light luggage the friends drifted away in the morning sunlight. For sometime, the old Boramma stood there staring at the diminishing figures in the east. When her eyes failed her, she got indoors. There were marks of elation on her face today. She was in deep meditation about the yet unapproved future daughter-in-law and the possible grandchildren. Sometimes Boramma did not fail to forget her sister's miserable end because of her indifferent daughter-in-law. Of course, she thought, her sister's fault was as much as the young woman's. Had she not troubled her son's wife, Boramma thought, the daughter-in-law would have not tortured her. Still many thoughts and feelings occurred to her senile mind. Harikrishna's memories too engaged her. This man was her brother who had settled down in the garden city of Pampapattan. He had only one son already married. Harikrisna's daughter-in-law was a perfect woman — obedient and virtuous. She was not only admired by her family, but by the whole neighbourhood. Like Savitri, she was a very good wife to her husband, and an ideal daughter-in-law to her parents-in-law and an affectionate mother to her children. So many pictures about ideal sons and daughters-in-law flashed in Boramma's fragile mind. However she was raised by an old tradition, she was reasonable enough to sacrifice anything for the sake of her kindred. Like Olly Dowden, this matron's nature was to be civil to enemies as well as to friends and grateful to all the world for letting her remain happy and alive.

Lakkappa and Kallappa went to Hubli in search of a bride. As they knew the address, they went straightway to the house of Subedar Neelappa and the latter welcomed them warmly. Since Lakkappa had informed him in advance, Neelappa had been ready to initiate the birdshot. Lakkappa and Kallappa sat together upon a luxurious sofa, which they had never seen earlier. Everything in the house looked impressive. The outsiders too looked smart. Then Neelappa, the retired Subedar invited those whosoever had to be present on the auspicious occasion.

'It's Lakkappa, my friend,' Neelappa introduced the tallest of the two to his men. The others simply saluted Lakkappa. Subsequently Kallappa was presented to the gathered as the prosperous bridegroom. Not much later than this, came there the bride in her golden attire. Then everyone turned his attention to her. Though she had dressed exquisite, the maid's skin colour was seen at least on her face. She was as dark as a Negro — a blackie. Kallappa, it seemed, had never seen such a woman. This was attributed to her mother's complexion. In this situation what one would have to think of her mother's colour? Really she was the darkest. Therefore, it was customary in Neelappa's house that whenever men came to see his daughters, he did not allow his wife come out. For her sake a big hole was made in a wall and the old woman was free to see her future son-in-law from that mysterious cavity.

'May I know your name?' Kallappa asked her politely.

'It's Sundaradevi,' replied she.

Meanwhile something irked Kallappa. This was the very contradiction in god's creation. Though her name was Sundaradevi, meaning the goddess of beauty, or the Miss Universe of modern times, she looked as if a clay of carbon.

'What's your education?' Kallappa asked her once again. In fact, this was his last question.

'I've got a B.A. degree.'

'Alright you may go in,' one of the gathered suggested her, lest, he thought, Kallappa would ask her many more questions.

Soon tea and snacks were served in goodwill and respect and the things moved to a finale.

'Well...We'll go sir,' Lakkappa said to Neelappa, while the latter called him inside and spoke to him something who knows what. Thereafter, the two figures left for another house in search of a better breed.

It was Guddalingayya's house where Lakkappa with his friend arrived after an hour or two. But in the absence of its housemaster, the landlady Shantamma arranged the brideshow. Of course, there was her brother to help her. Lakkappa who was familiar with them introduced the bridegroom to them all. Thereafter the girl was asked to appear on the spot before all the gathered as if she had blundered against their fate. This time the surprise for Kallappa was different. It was sure Kallappa was around thirty and he had an independent source of livelihood for his family. But to him Shantamma's daughter looked too old — say thirty-five or so. Already the scars that indicated overagedness had become visible on her face. Anyway there was an idea to marry a woman of his age for the sake of clear understanding and better gratification in Kallappa's mind, this woman fell below the line. More than that he thought that she might be a widow. Another thing that added to the foreboding was that she appeared to be domineering.

'May I know your name?' First she began here.

'I'm Mr. Kallappa.

'Are you in service?' asked she. It was, however, not her final question.

'Yea, I'm a bank clerk.'

'Good... Very good...What about your parents?'

'O! I've lost my father many years ago and my mother lives still.'

'Fine...'

Still many of her questions came and they came continuously. Though none of her questions was inconsistent to the occasion, her overage and fatbody were not to be overlooked. Then as a matter of custom, lunch was served. Believe it or not, everyone felt thrilled by the occasion. Shantamma told Lakkappa that he should ring her up the next day just in connection with the affair.

Finally when Lakkappa and Kallappa arrived at Mrs. Shantkumari's house, it was three o'clock afternoon. Shantkumari, a widow whose husband had been a Hindi Professor in Pampapati University, was a perfect lady. However, there was none from her husband's side to look after her, she managed everything with her brother's assistance. Lakkappa knew that Shantkumari had three daughters and all of them were of marriageable age. Hence, she had asked Lakkappa to help her in arranging their weddings. No wonder, presently she was glad since Lakkappa had come with a handsome happy-to-go-lucky-chap. Here as a mark of cordiality, tea was served even in advance. Now Shantkumari introduced her daughters to Kallappa after knowing him fairly well. What a fortune? She gave the bridegroom a splendid chance to see all her girls hoping that he might like one of them certainly. Gracefully next to these girls had sat Mrinalini, Shantkumari's youngest sister whose life had gone wrong because of her husband's pitfalls. Mrinalini was already a mother of two sons – yet happy of her fate. Presently she sat beside her sister's daughters just to facilitate the ceremony. But never she knew that the bride's attention would be focussed upon her alone.

Kallappa had sat comfortably and with him was his friend. One by one, as a public officer inspecting things, he saw the girls and saw Mrinalini. There he was a little confused. All ladies, no doubt, looked nice and beautiful. But Mrinalini whose *tali* he could not notice easily and as he mistook her to be one more daughter of the matron, looked to him very fascinating. Indeed, ever since he had born, he had never seen such a heavenly maid. So he cast his eyes upon that poor fellow only. No doubt, Mrinalini looked a measure prettier than any women.

'You may like anyone of the three,' Lakkappa put it jovially. He thought Kallappa was lucky enough in getting a handsome choice, which he had never seen in the past. This made him to believe that his friend would like to marry Sujata, Shantkumari's eldest daughter who too looked not less pretty than her aunt. Notwithstanding Lakkappa had already told it to Kallappa, the latter's fascination for Mrinalini increased. Admittedly he did not remember the fact that Shantkumari had only three daughters. Naturally this led to a wilderness.

'I like that madam very much,' pointing towards Mrinalini, Kallappa took everyone by surprise.

'No…no…She's my sister…' Shantkumari spoke a little upset. Kallappa's strange choice had shocked everyone. However Mrinalini's marriage with her husband could not run smooth, she was not a divorcee yet. Of course, she could remarry, Shantkumari, as a well wisher had decided her case just the otherwise. Since she had already two sons, Mrinalini too did not think of a remarriage. Under this circumstance, when she heard Kallappa's uncouth wish, rather afraid of the situation, Mrinalini hurried indoors. Really for a long time even she did not think of overhearing the ongoing conversation that was fierce in the hall.

Lakkappa who knew her tragedy enquired Shantkumari to clarify the case. Perhaps his intention was to settle down the affair if it could favour them both. Anyway he knew she was more than a widow and if she liked, he felt, she could marry someone. But he did not know that she had sons. Presently the problem of settling her sons was beyond any solutions. A little later, he heard that she did not wish for any conjugal bliss too.

'Has she taken a divorcee?' Lakkappa enquired the old woman.

'Not yet Lakkanna. Even she's two sons. However, we advised her for remarriage, because of sons, she doesn't like it,' Shantkumari made it crystal clear. But Kallappa was very much fascinated by her beauty. Her silk saree and sleeveless blouse might have aroused his desire to marry her at any cost. No surprise, he took not much time to make it clear.

'Madam if you don't mind, I'll marry her and take care of her sons,' he told to Shantkumari without anticipating the consequences. Nor did he think of his mother whether she could permit him to do so? Since her angelic beauty infatuated him, he was heavily bent upon to wed her regardless of the difficulties he could face in society. However, the matron was quick to understand the matter clearly. She thought further argument was pointless. So she assured Lakkappa that she herself would let him know her further decision. This was a clear indication that Lakkappa was not to enquire her further.

Lakkappa and Kallappa began their homeward journey. They spoke very less for a long time. But when they came their homes, they tried to read each other.

'Whom you liked most?' Lakkappa asked his friend enquiringly.

'I'd like to marry Mrinalini Lakkanna,' Kallappa was still in his old mood as if he was in Shantkumari's house.

'But she's two sons though her marriage is broken up. What can you do for them?' Lakkappa questioned him. Although he was not sure of facing the oddities and bearing the brunt of social dislike, Kallappa nodded him positively. Soon Lakkappa thought any further enquiry was pointless as Kallappa was suffering from love-sickness.

During the next week, Lakkappa was able to get the results of bride hunting business. He informed Neelappa and Shantamma about Kallappa's disinterest in their daughters, while he rang up Shantkumari to know whether Mrinalini will marry Kallappa.

But Shantkumari said 'no' as Lakkappa told the same to the other parties. This led him to a final overthrow.

Nonetheless, the next week their journey in search of a suitable bride began again. This time they went northward against the southward direction of the last time. This was done in consonance with a sage's advice that the bridegroom would get his woman in a northern village. The bus in which they sat was bound to Bijapur. They had to see a bride in the house of one of their friend's friends in Jamakhandi. This time the friends were optimistic as the sage had doubly blessed them. As it was a festival day, the bus was fully rush and neither of them got a seat. But on the way when an elderly person alighted a seat was vacated. However, soon a well-built man occupied it though Kallappa claimed it for himself as he had requested the woman who just got down from that seat. But Rudrappa the stranger was quite adamant. He resisted the opposition and sat upon it saying that he came from Hubli longstanding. But Kallappa was not a man who could lose his heart. So instantly he picked up a quarrel. Even there began a word to word fight between them.

'Get up! This's my seat,' said Kallappa angrily.

'No; never; I won't,' Rudrappa held the ground.

'Lo! Is it not the seat we got reserved,' Lakkappa tried to support his friend.

'Lo, tell me who put the bag first?' Rudrappa burst like a loin.

'Of course, it might be you, but before that, it was we who kept it reserved for us,' Kallappa argued reasonably.

'Yes…Yes…,' said the oldest of them sarcastically.

When the word to word fight between them reached an alarming stage, the conductor rushed there to settle down the score. This saved the situation as Rudrappa was shortly to be beaten up. Nor was Rudrappa less haughty in the matter either? Both parties looked equally strong. So when they were on the verge of exchanging blows, the conductor merely on account of

Rudrappa's oldage requested the other two to take patience until Ramdurg. He said at Ramdurg, many passengers were to get down. That was why the man in *kaki* silenced the wordfight. However, the discomfort between them continued as long as the annoyed persons did not get seats. So only at Ramdurg, the amusing hiccup ended.

The time the Bijapur bus reached Jamakhandi, Kallappa and Lakkappa were as silent as the other passengers. They were feeling well. But they did not talk to each other though all the three had rested in a single row. Nor was there any necessity felt either? Soon Kallappa and Lakkappa alighted. So did Rudrappa. The friends went to Krishnappa's house. Then to become five persons, an auspicious number, with his wife and daughter, Krishnappa took his friends to his friend's house where Kallappa could find his sweetheart as the holyman had predicted.

Unfortunately the time these persons went there, the master of the house was not at home. It seems he had gone somewhere. Anyway that did not matter. The landlady and her brother-in-law managed everything. Krishnappa introduced Laxmibai, Rudrappa's wife; Rekha, his only daughter; Murty, his son and Venkappa, his brother. But he did not say anything about Rudrappa. Nor did he mention his name? Presently they were busy in their immediate concern.

Rekha, for that had been the bride soon sat upon a chair. She looked a perfect lady. She was in her mid thirties — very beautiful and healthy. Her pretty dress, well-built body, fair complexion — all went in making her a belle. She bore a good character besides. Even like Kallappa, she had an M.A. from Pampapati University. Everyone in Rudrappa's house was fine.

However, people withhold their approval for sometime, Kallappa, a man of demoniac curiosity and hasty temperament declared it immediately. He told them he liked Rekha very much. Having heard this, Laxmibai, Venkappa, in fact, everyone of the family became gladder than he. Already Kallappa had asked questions and the way he did and she answered them had pleased one and all.

Oddly enough then like a bolt from the blue appeared Mr Rudrappa, the hero of that quarrel in their journey the previous day. He got indoors. On dressing he burst in the hall where the show had been still underway. Alas! He took Lakkappa and Kallappa by great surprise. Nor could the two believe that they had come to the very house of the man who, in spite of his own mistake, had humiliated them? At once there fell a deep silence. No wonder, amidst this, Krishnappa's work of introducing each other looked dry and dull.

'It's Rudrappa, the master here.'

'Oh!..oh!..Is it?' stammered Kallappa as if something suddenly befell upon him when he had not yet prepared to face it.

'O!.. My goodness!' Lakkappa exclaimed. He found everything unbelievable. They were brought to the house of a man, who by his words only, had beaten them. For a while, only that fierce wordfight disturbed the minds of the two. By the virtue of age, Rudrappa had been able to see them however with love and friendliness. He forget the quarrel. Nor did he think of hurting them either? Even he smiled upon them.

Kallappa and Lakkappa sat still. Good or ill, Kallappa had already given his consent to marry Rekha. Even he was not unhappy of that. Why should he worry of his father-in-law as the maid mattered him most? Thereafter sumptuous meals were served. In course of time, the things moved to a close. When Krishnappa made a move for departure, Rudrappa asked him for a closet. Then the other went into brief the glad things.

As everything is fair in love and war, the friends forgot the bizarre incident and found thrilled at the success. Good enough, when they began their back home journey, Rudrappa salaamed them. Equally Kallappa and Lakkappa could not help rising to the occasion. Though the whole affair was irksome yet it was amusing.

ooo

4
A POLICEMAN AND HIS GIMMICKS

'STOP! STOP! Lo! Rascal...Stop there,' cried Mr Timmayya, the police constable of Pampapati University Police Station. He was very angry when the lorry driver did not stop his vehicle, which was fully loaded and come from Andra Pradesh. Besides, the driver was speeding it recklessly, which as per the IMV Act was objectionable. Soon the lorry stopped abruptly. But the driver being familiar with police tactics sat silent. He did not come down to respect the man who represented the Government department in *kaki*. This naturally upset Timmayya who reddened with anger at the man inside glanced at the load with an inquiring gaze.

'Get down, I say,' thundered Timmayya.

'What for?'

'Wh...What for?' the police spoke in clenched teeth. He began burning. He asked him to produce his licence. Then dismayed of his pitfalls, the driver who had drunk fully instantly got down and displayed his records. He threw at the constable a glance of curiosity. Since the police went on checking them, the driver afraid of his drowsiness searched for a Rs. 100 note. No doubt, bribing was not uncommon at the Campus Station as anywhere else. All people knew that police were the most corrupt Government servants. For any mistakes — for lack of records, for transporting prohibited goods and passengers and for avoiding the eye of them — the lorry drivers were supposed to oil police. Nor was it considered wrong? No. Since, most of the times, the drivers committed mistakes and did many things besides, obviously they were at fault. On the pretext of carrying goods, they transported prohibited things and made money. Many mistakes they committed would have been avoided had they taken the slightest care. But they did not. So they did not observe traffic rules. Did they wear uniforms? Their licence and records were not renewed and not properly maintained. Even they drove their vehicles over or underspeed — ignoring traffic signs. So causing accidents. Not to speak of this, they were indifferent towards the state buses. Troubleshooters.

Timmayya, as he was wise and expert, found faults with the records as well as with the holder of it. Because of the driver's adamancy, he had already decided to teach him a lesson. This made the other stretch out a Rs. 100 note gleefully. But Timmayya refused it.

Since Timmayya stood like an electric pillar with no gestures for some time, the driver presuming that he was at fault picked out another currency of the same value. More the police turned cold, weaker became the driver. The matter was further worsened, when the police found him drunk too.

'Stupid fellow…drunken…Stop the lorry that side,' Timmayya burst firmly.

'Why sir?'

'You've drunk, haven't you?'

'Very less.'

'Less or little, doesn't matter. As the rule doesn't allow you to drive drunk, park the lorry there,' he shouted. Gradually he lost interest in the fellow. Obviously his purpose was to avoid him going in that state as much as to squeeze him.

'O! Something? What're the goods?' looking at the load, the police threw an enquiry again.

There was a pause.

Just the same, the driver did not speak. This increased Timmayya's doubt.

'You've also loaded the top. That's not permitted.'

'Yes sir.'

'Yes sir' is not a sufficient reply. Give reasons.'

'It's done in response to my boss's order.'

'Stupid Fellow... Does your boss come here to rescue you?' the police grilled the other sternly. Like a gor-crow, he moved here and there as if he was likely to check up the goods. This startled the other. As he had already alighted, even he was surmised to see huge buildings nearby. At once, a thought horrid came to him. He mistook one of the University structures for an SP's quarters. The dread in him was due to the fact that once he had been caught up by an SP for an illegal act and was beaten up. He thought had the police really inspected the lorry, he would have been arrested and his goods would have been confiscated. So the university buildings as he did not know them increased his fear. Already he knew the nature of PSIs and SPs. Therefore, he had decided not to repeat his earlier crimes. But he did not know what made him today to drink.

'Sir what're these buildings?'

'They're the university buildings.'

'Then that huge structure?' the driver waved his hands towards a vast heath on which a hill stood and on the hill stood a temple edifice.

'That's Pampapati Temple. D'you want to go there? Even though you go there, the god won't spare you from my clutches.' Remember, Timmayya smiled upon his pray.

Now the driver was at a crossroad. Neither he could bribe him as the other had already refused it nor he could run away leaving the vehicle to its own fate. Then suddenly he decided to try once again to oil the hand of police. He knew the police were very typical people. It was an old saying 'buttock is not a holy place and a police is not a friend.' Who knows what he has to face there because of the corrupt police, he thought. Police were police. Since they are spies, they cannot spare anyone — good or ill. Like a cathouse woman who spoils men by lifting up her legs, the police, he thought, could wreck any havoc. He knew their language was unofficial and decent people could not befriend them. Even people think it is below their dignity to associate with them. Sure some people of the Campus who had tasted the police hospitality would say that man must be free from these dangers — a police, a whore and a students' crowd. This is how people did not have a good opinion of the police.

Like the fluttering wheat, many bitter ideas occurred in the driver's naked mind now. Not latter than this he opened his inside pocket and picked up a five hundred rupees note. He was lucky, for, by this time, Timmayya too had decided to dispatch him. The latter's fear arose due to his boss's cross enquiries.

'Sir take it,' the shabby cabbie came forward humbly. His face was downcast to show his faults and low was his tone to indicate his obedience.

'Is it just a hundred rupees?' Timmayya thundered. The fault was neither's. The driver had given him a five hundred-rupee currency note, which Timmayya had mistaken for a hundred one. Great was his wonder when the other revealed it.

'Give me one more,' Timmayya turned greedy.

'I've no more sir,' the other put it plainly. The police was at the driver's mercy. The desire for money had made him so.

'Doesn't matter.'

'How can I give you more when I don't have any?'

'Rascal…I know you. Open the jacket pocket,' Timmayya forced his victim mercilessly.

'Sorry sir…Much is already given,' broke the other.

'O! Asshead…D'you know you've drunk also,' the police rumbled. His expectation was upto one thousand. So he turned a beggar.

When the driver gave him another two hundred rupees, the police was fully satisfied and he asked him for no more. Timmayya turned to his place eagerly pocketing his labourless earning. Happy of money he asked the driver to go away. He was wise enough to apprcciate the beauty of sensitive matters.

However, not many hours later another lorry came there. It was empty. So Timmayya did not show any interest. He had a morale. However, the people blamed the police, Timmayya felt, they had a work ethic. They did not ask the local drivers for money. Nor did they stop empty vehicles? Only the loaded lorries, distant lorries and lorries that carried prohibited goods would engage their attention. Often if the drivers were not in a condition to oil them they did not worry. In all, the police would work for the public harmony. This is how they had been sympathetic towards the channel of public life.

Thereafter an empty lorry came. With that came the Vice-Chancellor's car — very big, long and white in colour. It was exquisite in appearance. Whenever this car passed on the Campus roads many persons were scared of it. Even the aged professors did not like to be seen by the VC who used to scold them like anything. The VC would check everyone who came under his sway. Since he did not know his own respect, he hardly respected others' — good or bad. Therefore, people avoided him all the way — on the roads, in the departments and even about the streets in city. But the VC had adopted some shrewd means to keep people on strings. He had devised many rules such as people of one cadre had not to be seen in the company of others. He had asked them to be punctual even though they did not take classes. He would not allow people either to start or finish their say. O! He was rather a ball of fire. His most important gimmick to put people in fear was that his car was run on the campus though he did not travel in it. Thus he had turned the things to his advantages.

After the VC's white car, a jeep came. Soon another truck fully loaded or not, arrived there with a distorted board. In response to Timmayya's signal, it stopped. Soon the driver got down with his documents. He looked a huge figure in physic. His nose was slightly askew — face misshapen. His long and ruddy beards and whiskers were enough to terrify any civilised people. He looked like a man from a previous millennium. But he was timid enough to draw Timmayya's undivided attention.

The time the lorry stopped, Timmayya did not want to check his records.

'Give *mamula*,' said he. Soon even he saw the driver extending some loose notes which on counting did not exceed even a hundred.

'Not enough...'

'No more than this,' said the other giving him some notes. This made Timmayya happy and Timmayya returned to his place safe.

Timmayya was happy like a man who solved an eternal riddle. Naturally he was proud of his boss who had given him enough liberty to exploit victims. Besides, he knew his boss did not cross-question him over the money he used to get. This made Timmayya glad. Timmayya used this kind of money to enrich his home and farm instead of spending it on drinks and women. Actually it was very common to many police to fall for pleasures and get home empty handed. So their extra money would go to their kepts or to beerhouses. Indeed, they gambled away their black treasure.

Yes after ten minutes or so, Timmayya's boss arrived. With the Police Officer's jeep a van of Veerabhadrayya, a coconut plantation owner came. Soon Shindhe, Timmayya'a boss alighted and gave Veerbhadrayya a signal to go home. He did not forget to tell his friend that he would join him soon. The town knew both Veerbhadrayya and Shindhe had been thick friends. Their intimacy had grown over the years for the sake of mutual benefits. They would tour together; fall in revelry and enjoy things their flesh was hair to. Since Veerbhadrayya was thought to be the candidate for the next general assembly election, all people — the high and low — gave him much importance.

Soon Shindhe and Timmayya went to a nearby inn. Since there were no people, the higher officer was free to talk to his subordinate on any confidential matters. Timmayya briefed him about the amount till then he had received from drivers. Shindhe expressed his joy over it. They talked on subjects that mattered them valuable. Truly they were intimate. As Timmayya enjoyed his officer's perfect confidence, he talked to him frankly. His speech was amply clear. No surprise, Shindhe expressed his consent for whatever his fellow did. But he would also alert him about the *lokayukt* that would detect corruption cases. The constable would accept these suggestions gladly. In fact, Timmayya was a yes man. Soon tea was served and Shindhe left.

Timmayya's pride increased as the environment favoured him. In his mood of joy he would smile upon others. But the moments of his happiness did not last long. Presently he saw a lorry running overloaded. Another meekly followed it. Since Timmayya stood on the way to stop, the first halted abruptly. Of course, did the other. As per the constable's advice, the vehicles were parked on a side. The drivers who were familiar with Timmayya paid him their due respect. Just the same, they were glad to take their seats beside him.

'Last time you didn't pay me?' Timmayya asked the older of the two.

'I went empty.'

'Of course.'

'How could I bribe you when I myself fell short of money?' he replied. Surely he was a clever chap.

'Since many times we go without goods, you shouldn't press us,' burst out the fatter of the two. This fellow who sat beside the taller one supported him always. When Timmayya was a little bit hurt by this, one of the two burst out again.

'Sir my boss wants to know why we'd bribe you.'

This simply startled the police. None had asked him thus. So, for a moment or two, he sat frozen.

'Oh!...Good God...Does he want to know it? Let him come here...Rascal,' Timmayya started scolding. 'Only scoundrels question me like this...D'you know bastards that there're IPCs and MVAs? D'you think we act arbitrarily? We've rules and regulations. There're officers to look after these, and ministers control us. We never do anything at our will,' Timmayya stopped for breathforce.

Timmayya was grossly annoyed. The cabbies sat silent. Now occasional were their noddings. Despair had struck them and their faces turned downcast. Did the police stop scolding them either? Showing the book *The Motor Vehicles Act*, which contained Central Vehicle Rules, Timmayya went on hurling.

'See this is a book of law for you. It contains rules about your licence, vehicle records, court powers to disqualify the anomalies, traffic signs and signals, speedlimits, nature of parking, driving regulations and what not — everything...D'you know how much you've to pay when you ride without licence? When you don't stop for us? And when you violate traffic rules?' Timmayya went on even without waiting for their yeses and noes. In fact, like an irked animal, he was barking at them. Admittedly the drivers did not dare even to cough there and the police continued lecturing them.

'Well...D'you know that if you don't stop for us, you've to pay a fine of Rs. 70; and if you go without uniform, you'd pay a penalty of Rs. 150. Also there is a fine for your negligence of traffic rules and signs as well as to your recklessness...remember. When you're drunk, you can't ride and riding without uniform is a clear crime. I know you go with heavy loads and passengers, don't you? That's but illegal,' spoke Timmayya continuously while the poor fellows kept on nodding. Indeed, now they had realised the gravity of situation.

'We know it sir. But we didn't know all of it,' said one of the two downcasting his eyes.

'Oh!...Knowers of Rules...See how you contradict yourself. You say you know it, and at the same time, you say that you're ignorant of it...Nonsense.' Timmayya burst sarcastically.

Consequently each of the two drivers extended Rs. 100. But Timmayya rejected it outrightly.

'Stupid fellows...D'you know,' he began, 'there is an ethic even to bribe. See we've three adjustments — the first from

Re. 1 to Rs. 99; the second from Rs. 99 to Rs. 999; and the third from Rs. 999 onwards. I'm sure you can't come under the first category. So each of you must give me an amount not less than Rs. 500,' Timmayya broke for more money.

'Ex..excuse me sir. To…today our lorries're not carrying any rich goods and we can't pay you more,' pleaded the shorter of the two humbly.

'Even we fall short of pocket money,' the other supported his crony grumbling.

'But you speak a lot about law and order. D'you observe them either?' Timmayya closed his lecture on his so-called work ethics.

'Please finish the deal,' one of them requested and the other nodded meekly.

'How can I accept only half of the amount which I deserve best?'

'Next time we'll adjust it,' assured the cleverest of the two.

'Ha…ha…ha…This's your refrain always,' broke the police laughing.

'Not refrain sir, a promise,' the two spoke together.

'Alright,' said Timmayya, while he pocketed the money.

The drivers soon went off in a mood of joy to have troubled the police. But they did not know Timmayya was gladder than they.

It was 7 o'clock evening — the end of Timmayya's duty. Though he was firm in his decisions, the thrills of his heart forced him to leave for the colony of suburban woman. So he moved there.

OOO

5

VENKAPPA AND A CORPSE

WHEN MR. Venkappa, the traffic Controller of KSRTC Pampapattan came to the bus stand to attend to his duty on an August Saturday 1998, at once, what he saw was a crowd standing there in confusion. Naturally he wished to see the things. He was a man of big body, course hairs, wide forehead and plumpy cheeks. Venkappa was a big person but very crooked. All knew what kind of officer he was. Nonetheless, people addressed him sahib. His position helped him in commanding respect from the laity, and in no occasion, he knew, he was insulted. Having known his nature, everyone bestowed upon him some respect. But those who knew his baseness disliked him. Some people knew he was unthankful too. Admittedly his cheap end was to live comfortable. His wife, in this regard, though tried to chastise him had failed. His bestial passions made him neglect others. When he forgot his family, partly his relatives looked after it. Venkappa's extra-marital relationships had worsened his family peace and happiness. But his whores had controlled him — polishing always. No wonder, to manage a big family and at the same time to live happily, Venkappa saved no efforts to earn money. Consequently he never bothered of justice since his sole end was to lead a joyous life earning as much as possible.

Presently Venkappa got the news of somebody's death in the stand. He enquired a variety of passengers as well as watchmen as to how the man met his tragic end. But nobody gave him any right answer. If one said the ill-fated man died due to bouts of drinking, others would say he died in an accident. Still many others spoke anything as their whims directed.

Just the same, the talk of passengers was interesting. A passenger who came from Dandeli exclaimed, 'O! a gentleman's passed away here!' A kind man, he prayed god to bless the departed soul. Another person from Mysore uttered, 'God save him.' They muttered, 'he's died here in an unworthy place.' On the other hand, a woman who journeyed in the same bus, on seeing the man's ugly look, abused him. She touched her sunken face once, twice and thrice and uttered *santam papam*. Never, never, she said, she had seen such a spectacle in her life. She prayed god not for the sake of the dead, but for the sake of herself — for a safe further travel. She shuddered saying — 'it's terrible, terrible as the grave.' Not to speak of she was scared of death as much as children were scared of darkness. Presently she asked a fellow passenger whether the man had died in a bus accident. But the other expressed ignorance. This made her even not to alight for recess. Likewise a fellow who got down from a Bijapur bus was shocked at the spectacle — a disaster. No doubt, soon he grappled down. Suddenly someone who had been rather friendly took him to a nearest hospital. On administering medicine, this man got recovered. According to the doctor, he told him that on seeing the bloodstained corpse, reminding his brother's murder the previous year, he lost his heart. Anyway he was discharged. Similarly there was another aged woman who was also badly affected by this. She told her daughter, 'see how he's died here.' She was dismayed of life's darkness. 'O! God what about his family!' at once exclaimed she. Her daughter who did not lose her heart burst, 'god's there. He'll save all.' 'Anyway,' the older woman continued, 'a middle aged man dying is something untimely.' However, Gangu, her daughter did not speak concertedly. 'Yea, mummy he lost the world as much as his family lost him. But the society can't worry over this.' She continued, 'we're all mortal and one day or other, we've to die because of god's curse, haven't we?' Her reply was philosophically coloured, while the unhappy mother sobbed. The latter recollected how her husband's brothers disturbed her while getting the ancestral property divided. How could she forget a relative's attempts to share her? –A poor widow. Of course she faced the odds bravely, those worldly fetters had sapped her vigour. Not much later than this people saw tears trickle down from her wrinkled face and Gangu noticed her mother's extreme sympathy. Meanwhile, a bus without noticing the crowd came fast and dashed to some bystanders. As a result, a quarrel between the driver and the wounded broke out. It grew both in intensity and time. Only when a police appeared there, it subsided. The constable also tried to disperse the mob. The time I saw the dead, the crowd was gradually melting. My wife too burst out in a sympathetic vein. She said, 'see often you go to Gulbarga without reservation. If you die on the way,' she said, 'your condition will be just the same.' Though it was illogical, it hurt me. So I could not bear her talking of my end. The next moment I took no time to console her saying tha: god will protect us. 'That's true. Anyway, be careful,' she added lovingly.

Though the man had died, as some predicted, at 11 o' clock the previous night, still there was none to care the corps. The controller had thought that some relatives, or those who knew the dead man, would be looking after it. Once he saw the ugly body, Venkappa did not think of going there again. Not later than this, when an officer, mostly of education department suggested him a contributory funeral, the Controller expressed his helplessness. 'What can I do for it, let his people come,' he replied unkindly. So in all, first Venkappa did not take any interest in the affair. After all, events like deaths, quarrels and knifings were very common in public places.

It was a festival day. Everyone was glad to celebrate Dipavali with pomp and glory. Even the stand scavengers were nowhere to be seen. So no peons attended to their duty on one or another pretext. The number of clerks was negligible. Even the Controller could not come there was he not warned by his higher authorities. Today knowingly or unknowingly, to the misfortune of his family if not to his, or on merciful god's invitation, the stars had caused this man an ignoble death. However, the delay in his demise hurt most of the passengers. In this way, the day passed on, while the shadows of tall buildings fell down at eventide. Still nobody came and the crowd went away. However, buses came there every now and then. With each new bus many passengers alighted. Got down or got up or sat still, they talked of the dead only. Every time the response to the dead was a mixed one. Some would bless him, while others would curse him seeing his ugly make up. On their exercising of imagination, some of them would guess the nature of his death. They also cursed his relatives.

The situation turned tense when the wrath of passengers, shopkeepers and staff, turned towards the Controller. All alike blamed him. They thought he should have looked into the matter and arranged the dead man's funeral. Some countrywomen displayed their characteristic hatredness in hating the authority by knuckling their fingers. Some would say, 'che, che, it'd have not happened here,' while most others began cursing the Controller for the negligence.

Admittedly when it became dark, some ex-college students who had gathered there decided to do something about it. 'The best way for this,' they talked of, was to persuade the Controller to arrange the dead man a contribution burial. Accordingly, they met him and on their strong persuasion, Mr. Venkappa changed his mind to deal with the case. However, he was perturbed by the gravity of task. 'How to collect money' was his great problem. Luckily an old idea occurred to him. He remembered how a village official had collected money for the funeral of an orphan. No doubt, Venkappa too had contributed something towards that. This made him to call Tatya, his peon, and came in the peon at once. Soon Venkappa asked him to bring a tin.

'What for sir…?' asked the peon to whom Venkappa's ways looked strange. But the officer's furious gesture silenced him. By the time, a tin was brought, Venkappa himself wrote a label in bold letters — **PUT MONEY FOR BURIAL**. No doubt, the request was modest. Soon the label was attached too. The box was big enough to consist much money as Venkappa had manipulated. Tatya under the direction of his master put the tin on a stool near the dead. Venkappa saw that the tin was kept in such a place that all could notice it and the label looked appealing.

However, the number of passengers standing or passing by was first negligible, soon the box for money was exquisitely placed there, the crowd increased. People gathered there enthusiastically in a bid to see the new measure. None hurried first to drop any coins but to take a look at the box. Admittedly people rushed there to behold the crowd. Even the passengers who were not supposed to alight, got down to witness the scene. Fortunately some people began dropping coins and the rich put currency notes. Now the spectacle turned evocative. Most of the crowd stood then not to see the stinking corpse, but to see the growing gathering. One of the bystanders, with a mischievous look, then joked at his friend to put some money, otherwise, if he died, he said, none would lift his corpse. This naturally brought many to their senses. Consequently the standing people who were dropping money increased. Even the passengers, who sat in buses, came down to show their sense of charity.

Things, rightly or so, were in favour of Mr. Venkappa, the 'arranger.' The amount of money being collected upto 6 o' clock in the evening grew large. Meanwhile, the sun descended down in the Western sky and his golden rays diminished. The crowd of passengers gradually thinned near the dead as that began stinking. Someone buttoning his pant at a toilet talked of the Controller's inordinate delay. 'Though much money,' he said, 'is collected for the decent burial, the work is not yet begun.' The other replied, 'maybe the bloody chap desires more money.' Indeed, this was the reality.

When there were hardly a hundred people around, Venkappa asked his peon to fetch the filled in tin to his room. The servant did what he was told. People saw the peon carrying the tin inside. Somebody said, 'who knows the money will be rightly utilised.' Others as my friend said me murmured, 'if he misuses it, he'll incur the wrath of god.' But a fellow being questioned the very idea of divine justice.

The tin was obviously heavy. Venkappa asked Tatya to categorise the denominations. The peon did it though mechanically. Venkappa was happy to get a huge amount even in doing a bad job. Besides, he knew, people would admire him to have done a charity work. But he did not know they already knew his evil nature.

Presently Venkappa himself counted the money. In all he found Five Thousand Eight hundred Sixty-Five Rupees. He did not however, count the small units like five and ten paises. They were, as Tatya said later, twenty-five rupees, which he got as his tip. But Tatya could not know how much money was contributed and what percentage of the bulk remained with his boss. A poor fellow. He only knew he got 25 rupees, while his boss had a big share.

'Go to the house of Subbya and Lakkya and ask them to come to bury the dead body of the stand,' said Venkappa emitting clouds of smoke with his cigar. 'Tell him to come at once with their bier.'

'Yes sir,' replied Tatya. With his reply his presence gone. As the officer was aggressive, not only the peon but many of the stand were scared of him. They lacked a fortitude to question his unruliness. This way Venkappa controlled the people one way or other.

The time Tatya came to Subbya, with Lakkya, his uncle, Subbya was skinning an animal. He was happy about it as it was a healthy beast. No doubt, he wanted to feast its meat soon.

'Oh! Lakkanna and Subbanna, the Saab wants you,' Tatya cried in a bated breath.

'First let's know what for,' replied Subbya, the more aggressive of the two.

'A dead body is lying in the stand and he wants you to bury it soon,' said the bony fellow waving his hand towards the stand.

'Who does such work today?' said Lakkya piercing flesh.

'Why you worry he pays you,' Tatya encouraged him.

'Of course. Since we're busy here on this day, we'll do it tomorrow. Tell the Saab,' told Subbya.

'That won't do,' Tatya heaved a sigh of tension.

Since he was authorised, Tatya went to Kokka, a private scavenger. This fellow hated Subbya as well as Lakkya, because in his pride of government job, Subbya had become haughty. However, Tatya briefed him the matter. Kokka accepted the job overjoyed hoping he would do a bus stand work and get some money too. Soon he gathered some of his able-bodied kinsmen to lift the corpse. In all, his group consisted of five members whose names were Kyath, Thakka, Putta and Venk. So without any loss of time they rushed to the stand with a wild bier.

Meanwhile, it was seven o' clock. Mr. Venkappa after pocketing Rs. 5000 safe for himself came out with Rs. eight hundred to brief Kokka about his duty. If he properly buried the body, the Controller said, he would give his group Rs. 400. But Kokka pleading for more expressed his displeasure. Then moved by the appeal made by Kokka et al, Venkappa agreed to pay them Rs. 500. This made them happy and contented.

Kokka and his group took off the body towards god's acre. The small procession, say of ten people did not include any relatives or friends of the dead. However, some beggars followed it in the hope of getting some alms, which as per Venkappa's order Tatya had carried. This was done as a matter of custom. Thus the bier was carried to the graveyard, a mile or so away from the stand.

Hardly later than the corpse was about to be buried, Subbya's party hurried there with canes, sickles and shovels. Loudly one of them cried, 'Lo! Sons of bitch stop it.' 'O! Sons of owl, who said you to do our bus stand work,' added another. Controlling his fists, Subbya broke, 'Stop! Bloody fellows.' Then taken aback, Kokka and his men all stopped burying. Soon Subbya's party began to exchange blows.

What a wonder! Kokka was not yet clear over the hustle.

When Subbya told it, Kokka took no time to boast of the controller's order. 'Why you lifted the corpse of our stand?' Lakkya couterargued. Kokka said, 'it's the government stand,' while Subbya began beating him. Still another cried, 'it's your enmity that led to do this work of ours.'

Already the savage fight between the gangs of Kokka and Subbya was going on. Everyone related to the parties or not was alert about it. None remained a neutral territory excepting the stand peon. Already the poor beggars had flown to save their souls. Tatya too moved to a safer distance. The two parties by this time were at a terrible fight over the issue of their fundamental rights. This took no time even to frighten the passers-by. Hence, no civilised person dared to meddle for them. Though a police was looking at them, he did not come there. Nor did he report the matter to his station either? He might have thought that such things were common in the metropolitan city Pampapattan. However the darkness thickened, the low class people were busy in throwing sticks, beating each other and screaming in themselves. Subbya then threw his machete to Kokka's brother which unfortunately cut his own son's head. Enraged by this, Kokka pulled the bier for a wooden peace and in a single stroke beat Subbya to death. Likewise, Subbya's men fell down due to fatal wounds. The time Subbya died, three of his men had already joined the rank of the fallen. Kokka too received several injuries. But Kyath was a clever chap. He held the ground carefully. So was Thakka. The remaining three persons of Subbya's party quickly fled away while five were there bleeding on the ground.

Indeed, on account of this gruesome event, the next day *Deccan Herald*, a major south Indian newspaper sold very well in the city. The papers in the regional languages had already exhausted by the noon. A column in the English daily ran thus :

A Brutal Quarrel, 4 Died, 7 Injured

> A heinous quarrel took place between two low class parties over the issue of who should bury a corpse which was lain in the bus stand, Pampapattan. As a result, 4

men died, 7 were severely wounded and many got considerable injuries. It was a brutal incident over a small issue of burying never happened in the history of mankind.

ooo

6
FATE

'OH! BABU come here. Don't trouble him. Let him get in,' Manappa cried impatiently.

'No daddy I don't like him. I'll teach him a lesson. Nonsense,' Babu, an arrogant boy spoke with utmost enmity.

The man who was just got rid off from Manappa's cottage was none other than Babu's uncle Rayappa who had come there from the nearest village Malgudi, which was known for sheeprearing. He was known for his adamancy by developing over the years a sort of indifference towards Manappa's family in persuasion of an old feud. But Manappa, a very good person neglected the old relationship that went wrong. He thought that the rivalry that existed between his father and Rayappa's went off with them. Broad-mindedly Manappa stood for a healthy change in the family tradition. However, the vying continued by Baburao, his first son, who was otherwise known as Babu affectionately. This Babu was a young man of twenty-five, well built but illiterate. He was fair in the highest with curly hair very fair — brave but untamed. Whenever he lost his temper, he could get wild to such an extent that he might beat the other to wounds. His only virtue was that he would help those who believed him and appreciated his valour. Thus everyone in the hamlet knew him. No doubt, to avoid any ill-will, people appreciated the beauty of his bravery and the things went smooth.

One day Somu, the younger brother of Baburao went to Rayappa'a home in Malgudi. Rayappa's daughter was taken aback by his appearance, for Rayappa, they thought, did not wish Babu's brother visit them. Immediately the timid neighbours enquired Mayavva, Rayappa's daughter about the arrival of an unwanted clansman.

'He'd have come here to get his money back,' Mayavva replied her neighbours with an air of superiority.

'Is he not Babu's brother?' a frightened voice came.

'Yes.'

'Why Somu's come here?' an oldman asked Mayavva losing the presence of his mind.

'Can't you understand daddy? She's already told us that he's come here for money,' burst out his son.

'Doesn't matter,' Mayavva spoke calmly.

Their curiosity about Somu's mission deepened by the shabby appearance of the boy, who, like his brother, was very strong, tall and well built. His dark-coloured dress seemed darker due to the shade created by the falling sun.

Somu who was till then distant, arrived at the rugged hut of Rayappa. But he did not find his uncle. Instead he saw there a group of people that included his daughter.

'Why you've come here?' Mayavva remembering the old fued enquired.

'Don't worry, I've not come here to rape you,' the boy spoke smiling upon her.

'O! D'you have that guts?' Mayavva challenged him jovially.

'Yes, very much,' Somu exchanged word for word.

'Shall I think you've come here to pick up a quarrel with us?' the only female figure of the house burst doubtfully. The neighbours were in a state of confusion. The oldman was unhappy over the presence of a hostile person. His son and a boy were gaping at the stranger. Meanwhile a gammer hurried to the hut grunting.

'Nonsense, you always think of quarrels and nothing more,' Somu shouted at his opponent.

By this being pacified, Mayavva asked him to get indoors. Somu relaxed outside until she brought him a mug of water and he was asked to wash his face. Later he went inside to relax.

During this time nothing was more interesting than the immature neighbours' scuffle outside, as they were in a muddle. However, the old man withdrew being convinced of the situation that there was no danger in Somu's arrival. The boys too went off humming folk songs. Soon Mayavva tidied up the house and kept the things proper. She prepared some special food for the relative. The gammer, who failed to understand the situation, asked Mayavva whether she could help her. Good the girl accepted her assistance. In collaboration, the two women of different ages cooked some dish and hurriedly the younger of the two brought a plate of it to Somu, who rested outside in a place where mosquitoes were in abundance. A dog, which was beside him, began to bark, while there was a cat playing. However, unperturbed by the externals, Somu noticed the old hut and its dilapidated position. Indeed, the arrogance of its inhabitants for him was amusing.

Mayavva came out suddenly as if she rushed out from a hibernation period. She asked Somu to have meals. But the latter postponed the matter. He simply nodded and sprang upto see the grown up girl. His idea was that she could be a good match to his brother. Though the family relationship worsened over the years, Somu wished his brother should marry her and keep up the tradition unbroken.

'Since you're tired of journey, you may dine now,' the lady asked him fervently.

'Ok, what special food you've done?' he asked her pleased, tidying up his hair to look smart.

'Since it's a festival, we've prepared sweats,' told she to him laughing. Hardly later than this, the oldie who was indoors so far, rushed out. She looked ugly due to full of wrinkles on her face and body. But being still robust in health, she was quick tempered. She was called gammer affectionately. Her two sons, who went to a pilgrimage had never returned home. Besides, her husband, who died a long ago, had not left her any substantial property. By doing a variety of works, she pulled on her life. As none was there to look after her, she had maintained a cordial relationship with Rayappa. Now she was there to know whether Mayavva was in love with Somu or with his brother. As a result, she was more interested in inspecting her behaviour than in helping her.

When Mayavva described him the nature of sweets, Somu desired to dine. His wish to take meals with his uncle melted away at Mayavva's mellow voice. Admittedly she placed a plate of meals before him.

'O! You've so much. The preparation should've engaged you a long time,' Somu spoke to her smiling.

'No, I've not prepared it for you alone, but for the whole family,' Mayavva burst in a liquid tone, while she adjusted her saree on her breast. Somu, who so far did not notice her body, glanced at it when he found a chance in the cottage. At the same time, the oldie, who stood in a corner, would glance at him occasionally.

'The *Kadabu* is very tasty. I think the lady, who's prepared it must also be so,' he burst out with a broad smile.

'The item must be tasty, but it's not prepared by me,' Mayavva spoke teasingly.

'O! Then I've mistaken. Then what you've prepared?' Somu asked her for chatting.

'Only the *ladus* and nothing more,' Mayavva added it with a quick laugh.

'Anyway *ladu* is like you — round and beautiful,' now there was a change in Somu's continuation of talk. Gradually he found more interest in her than in the food. The visit certainly helped him to develop a fascination for her.

All this while the gammer was in a state of embarrassment. Presently she learnt that Mayavva did not love Somu. Besides, Mayavva's sense of superiority indicated her dislike for Manappa's family. The oldie was glad because she wanted her to marry her brother's son who though aged thirty had failed to get a bride. She knew he was not an eunuch though people called him. Merely for this only, she was Rayappa's neighbour. She also kept her relationship with them in harmony.

'Who's there? Come out quickly to save the child,' cried a shabby man outside at this time. A bullock was running panicky beside a child near the hut. The man thought that the untamed animal might crush the baby. In turn, soon an elderly person in the vicinity eased the hustle.

'Daddy come in,' Mayavva asked her father, who just arrived there.

'O! Has he come?...Good,' Somu spoke.

'Be alert, he may scold you,' for the first time, the woman in rags grunted.

But Somu did not heed her.

'What're you doing there? Who're there in the house?' Rayappa asked Mayavva sharply. Rayappa was a middle-aged man of challenging temper. His talkativeness made the cottagers call him wordie. However, his comic gestures and boastfulness had made him a jovial figure in the whole heath.

'Somu's come and I'm with the gammer,' the maid answered her father in a calculated manner.

'Why he's come? What's the matter?' Rayappa spoke heavily. His words were emotionally charged.

'Better you ask him. But I don't think he's come here with a bad air,' the daughter replied fearlessly.

Annoyed by these words, Somu maintained a bit of silence. He thought patience was a mark of wisdom. So he did not increase the heat though he did not know how much light he could bring to the two strife-stricken families. Meanwhile Rayappa greeted the peace-loving nephew and turned a little sober. He put out his dirty dress, splashed water to his face and came to the sofa where Somu relaxed gracefully.

'How're you boy? What's the matter?' enquired he.

'Uncle I'm well. Presently I've come here to give you a message from my father. He wants his money back you owe him,' Somu detailed the matter.

'What's the crisis for Babu's father?' the elder cross-examined.

'No problem as such but he's in need of money. So he's asked you to return his amount,' the boy repeated.

'Is it the matter? But I'm not having any money now,' the elder expressed his helplessness.

'You can pay whatever amount you've now.'

'No, I don't have any.'

'Then he'll turn unhappy.'

'Of course. But tell him that I'll pay him at the time of *Ugadi*,' Rayappa suggested the littleun an alternative.

'Okay.'

'What about your meals? Let's have it. Today we've sweets on account of the festival,' Mayavva's father asked the boy lovingly.

'I've already got it. Now I'd like to go home as daddy's asked me to return home soon,' the young man got up to return.

'Well; tell Manappa to chastise Babu. He's becoming a boor these days. You know how he insulted me last week,' Rayappa said it with a sense of displeasure.

'Don't worry. Now he's okay,' Somu concluded bidding them an adieu.

It was late afternoon when Somu got back home. The sun was still fierce, while people's diurnal activities were not yet ended. Unfortunately on coming home, Somu found his father ill. It was at this time Manappa summoned Babu for an urgent discussion. Soon the two sons sat there in despair.

'Did you bring money?' asked Manappa.

'No daddy. He didn't give it, as he says, he's not in a position to return it immediately,' Somu finished his say.

'Does he want to give back our money or not?' Babu burst wildly.

'Why you worry. He'll give it back,' Somu pacified his brother.

'It doesn't matter. Anyway we'll adjust,' Manappa advised his sons. 'But the purpose,' continued the old man, 'for which I've summoned you here is different. You know I'm aged. You've also lost your mother. Everyone knows you can't cook yourselves daily, as you have to work in the field. Therefore Babu, you must marry this year,' Manappa dumped a matter and waited eager for a reply.

However, Babu sat confused. So was his brother. For some time they could not appreciate the old man's wisdom. If Babu thought he was not sure of getting married soon, Somu looked nervous. In fact, Babu did not know whether Mayavva would marry him.

'Yea daddy let Babu marry this year. Anyway Mayavva is a good match to him. Her father will also approve this,' Somu justified the cause.

'I too suppose so,' Manappa agreed to Somu's view with gestures. His face was anxiety-stricken yet. Already bent in body, he did not like to die irresponsible. Therefore with so much of decision, he had proposed the matter.

There fell a deep silence.

Babu remained shy and silent. He did not haste to approve his father's point. Not to speak of this, he was also unaware of the responsibility of married life. Yet he knew the matter was of utmost significance.

'I'll marry next year. Let Somu marry this year,' replied he.

'It doesn't look nice,' the old man burst. 'Unless you, the elder in the family marry first, how can he, still a boy do so?' Manappa said reasonably.

'Yes, yes; you're right,' Somu nodded admiring the old man's stance.

'If then the situation is so, I'll marry first,' Babu agreed. 'But who's the bride?'

'You'll marry Mayavva,' smiled the oldest of them.

'Definitely,' Somu poked his nose.

'We'll ask him. If he doesn't agree, we'll go for another bride,' Manappa replied calmly.

So they decided the course of events. Soon each of them left for his business of the day. Manappa sent Somu to Malgudi for enquiring Rayappa over the proposal. Even the boy came with a positive nod. Rayappa had agreed to give his daughter though he was not happy with Babu. Subsequently Manappa and his friends fixed the day for discussion.

One day all the happy people gathered there. They fixed up April 10 as the wedding day. Meanwhile, the day and date of marriage were duly informed to the bridal party. After a week or so, Manappa's men went to Malgudi for the engagement ceremony. Every young and old, rich and poor of the hamlet gathered there as usual. Women gathered inside the house, while all men gathered under a big neem tree. The whole atmosphere was filled with joy and pleasure. All were happy. The children themselves engaged in house decoration; the elders were busy in reception and others were engaged in food preparation and exchanging greetings. The members of Manappa's family and his neighbours mingled with other party. Since Babu was reluctant to encounter his uncle due to the earlier accident, he sat beside his friends enjoying fruits brought for the occasion, while Somu was helping his people to get food. All the same, Manappa was busier elsewhere. Within the next hour all finished their dinner and the elders gathered under a shady tree for haggling over wedding expenses.

'The dinner's well arranged for you,' one of Rayappa's men spoke in a boasting manner.

'It's common everywhere for this kind of ceremony,' an

associate of Manappa replied without waiting for his friend's nod. It was his counterargument.

'Don't harp upon it and instead come to the point,' the wisest of the group warned them.

'What's your presentation to the bridegroom?' An elder of Shivagudi, Manappa's hamlet enquired.

'What's your demand?' Asked the man who boasted of the dinner just a short while ago.

There was a silence.

'We won't give you any dowry but full dress to the bride,' Rayappa said shaking his head. 'I'll buy as many dresses as she wants and you buy as many dresses to Babu as he likes.'

'How about marriage expenses?' enquired Manappa.

'I'll bear it. But you've to attend it on your own,' grunted his counterpart.

'That won't do,' Manappa expressed his inconvenience.

The discussion continued heated. Soon in the presence of three elders both the parties agreed to bear the expenses of each other's dresses. This, in fact, was the settlement of all things.

Soon a lunch for all was served. All the people from Shivagudi started to leave for their village. Rayappa's family members gave them a hearty look and his daughter Mayavva, who stood diffidently at a distance till then became overjoyed. A few of the womenfolk noticed her looking at Babu. She was no less thrilled during the festive occasion. So was her mother extremely happy, for her daughter was to marry her brother's son. Soon the outsiders took leave, while Rayappa and his men bid them a hearty adieu.

During the next month the leaders of Manappa's clan asked him to purchase dresses for the bridegroom. So Manappa sent Somu to Rayappa for bringing the dresses and the receipts for an inspection. He did it, as he had doubted Rayappa's credibility.. Really Rayappa too did not buy his daughter dresses worth of Rs. 10,000. This infuriated Babu. So he went for an enquiry.

But Rayappa was not prepared to answer his future son-in-law. Thus the situation turned tense. When they could not control themselves, soon a word to word fight began between them only culminating into blows. Meanwhile the hurt Rayappa declared that he would not even give his daughter. This was too much for Babu and the latter hit his opponent hard. Bleeding began at once and the bystanders were not strong enough to control Babu, the tiger there. A little later there also appeared three men in *kaki*. They were the policemen of Pampapati University campus. No wonder, soon Babu was arrested while he was at a loss to know the latest development. Nor were there any people to rescue him? As a result, he was taken to the Campus jail, which was located in the nearby woods.

Thus, passed a year or so.

One day Babu found the jail condition repulsive. Now he realised his mistakes. A sense of regret and remorse found a way. He thought it was foolish on his part to beat his uncle. He felt he himself got into problems. Regret paid way to repentance. His thought about his old and ailing father and his love for Mayavva made him totally unhappy. But his aggressive nature did not allow him to despair. Somehow he managed to come out of the shackle of mortification. Though disheartened, he gathered his strength and thought over the plans of escaping. His desire for Mayavva encouraged him to return home by any means. At last, he bent some iron rods of the jail and when it was still dark, he escaped away.

Soon Babu landed in a thick woodland known for its wilderness. Anyway the fear of bears struck him, he took no time to run away to an unknown carttrack.... He found a mango tree there. Already hungry, he ate as many mangoes as he could. No sooner he was about to alight the tree than he noticed a tiger glancing at him. Terrorstruck Babu at once climbed up further. He saw the tiger very much coming. It stood there at the foot of tree planning to catch him. Presently Babu was totally frightened. He felt he had been at least safe in the jail but here his life was at stake. So several ideas hit him. Even he cried but only to increase the tiger's wrath. Nobody could rescue him. So no salvation. Clenching his teeth, he improved his grip. Almost a day passed. But the tiger stood there still — waiting. This made him loose all his hopes for living. So unhope. Thereafter, luckily he found some noise. Some smoke in a nearby ridge. Predicting the noise for danger, the tiger took to its heels making Babu get a lease of life. When his fear was over, he got down and ran safe in the direction wherefore he had come. Not much later than two hours of running, he noticed a fine bungalow. Naturally his heart beat for some human consolation. So he entered the mansion for some food. After a due enquiry, he was given these things too. A careful Babu avoiding all doubts got a humane treatment for a day.

The next day morning, exactly at the same time he had escaped from the jail, Babu found the very man who caught hold of him at Rayappa's house. Quickly he ran helter-skelter. But his fate took its own course. Soon he was arrested on the ground of escaping besides dowry charge. Thereupon he was taken to the jail — same place and same food. The next day he had a dream and in his dream he saw his brother marrying Mayavva. The loss of freedom and more so, the imaginary or real loss of Mayavva whom he had held dearest made him lose all interest in life. So in the morning of the next day, he found himself lifeless in a small noose of rope.

ooo

7 ROBBERS AND THEIR MISCHIEF

WHEN THE door was knocked hard Swaminathan and Rukmini were fast asleep. Ravi and Kumar, his two children were placed in beds beside them. Although his beautiful house in Ramanager was well fenced and tightly constructed, a Naxalite gang at that fatal hour had arrived. When another knock rather harder sounded upon, Swaminathan got up certainly to see the situation though it was past midnight. The dogs began to bark and jackals howled in the distant woodlands. But none in Ramanagar was awakened and the members of his house were not an exception to this. Besides, as this house was at the fag end of Ramanager — very close to the jungle — it was advantageous to decoits to loot it at any time. However, nobody came to Swaminathan for a help. Be it known, many times Swaminathan too did not help his neighbours and he did not go to their rescue. Therefore at this time though a few of his close neighbours knew his house was going to be robbed, they did not desire to help him. To their dislike of him, added were his haughtiness, his wife's unusual pride and their total superiority.

The leader of robbers turned wild. When Swaminathan did not go forward to open the door due to his fear, they turned annoyed. Indeed, they were very bold. They were Naxalite who had come from the adjoining state of Swarnandhra Pradesh. They had a sizeable organisation; they got support from wealthy people; and their link with Government spies was strong. In fact, they enjoyed the confidence of local MLAs, MPs and Ministers. Being large in numbers they had vehicles, private spies and safety measures. Their connections were countrywide and they were a great force like the Thugs of 1820's and 1830's who were subdued by Lord William Bentick.

'We decoits've come here to loot your house,' a brave voice from outside was heard.

'Open the door and give your precious articles and whatever money you have,' like a death knell came another voice.

'We don't harm you or trouble,' so sounded the third.

This vice assured Swaminathan a feeling of life security. But he did not believe these voices. The question what guarantee was there troubled him. Therefore, he began to make a bell to a police station and in turn the decoits heard the phone sounds too.

The robbers who stood outside were ten in all. Three of them were very close to the door who just spoke in half Kannada and half Telugu, the Dravidian languages. In fact, their voice was not recognisable. For identification, were they well dressed either? They were in black dress and wore masks. Only the below portion of their faces was seen. They wore half pants, tea shirts and black goggles. They had worn shoes. They had no other clothes, facial gestures and physical features for tracing their disposition. Like Hitler's army all looked alike. They walked on half heels to avoid identification and produced they minimum sounds. All sorts of weapons were with them — knives, pistols and tools for cutting, drilling and the like and some chemicals to tackle enemies. Just the same some of them stood on the road, while some, in the lawn and near the highway to give them signals. Besides, most of them engaged to looting. Their vehicle was kept somewhere near the industrialised part of the town.

Not much later than this the robbers dashed a huge stone to the door. Suddenly fell the door broken down. Alas! Swaminathan was greatly embarrassed. He fell off when a robber slapped him with utmost force. The huge door had already fallen down in a dilapidated condition glorifyng the wealthy man's sin. This alarmed Rukmini who was sleeping. As she was much interested in sexuality, after the intercourse at night, as usual, she had slept naked. No clothes to speak of adored her. Besides, she was very beautiful and she was proud of it. This unusual nudity added its own mite to the current event. But the robbers, who cut telephone connection and took care of outside dangers, did not bother about her beauty. What mattered them was treasures and valuables of utmost importance. They were very swift in accumulating them. The time Rukmini tried to put on a cloth, the robbers stopped all lights. To avoid her noise, they opened the adjacent room where I was sleeping. I was in that rented room for my B.A. education. The robber, who took care of her stopped her by putting a piece of cloth in it, lifted her and threw her in the room where I was asleep. This at once startled me. Though like Kumbakarna I was asleep, I got up incessantly to start a light. But I could not believe what was placed on me with an utmost silence. When I really put on the light, I saw the celestial belle — all in golden hue. I simply wondered at the cloth in her mouth. After dumping her down there, the robbers had closed the doors outside.

'What a beautiful woman!' I wondered myself. But she signed me to get up and help her husband or her signs might have informed me to make efforts to call the neighbours. No doubt, I was at a loss to understand her gestures. However, I was helpless since my room door was bolted from outside.

Rukmini looked very lovely. Her plumpy body was wholly seen. More radiance was added to her then. I did not know whether I should close my eyes or wink not. But I did then what the hour permitted me. Her breasts were round and they looked like fresh apples. She was blue-eyed and shone radiant. Red as coral were her lips; and her teeth shone elegant. Like a dark-eyed heavenly maid, she was seen in the red light. None could deny this description if he saw her then. Slender was her waist and her limbs well shaped. In my mind I could not help thinking whether she was a real Rukmini I saw daily or she was a Krishna's Rukmini. Like a celestial *apsara,* she sat beside me. However, she had the rug covered around her, the black hair on her golden triangle stood like curly wool. And indeed, it was for the first time I saw an exquisite woman utterly fine. O! I was overwhelmed.

Meanwhile, she made me some more signals which I could not understand. Presently she was not shy of my seeing her, for she was very much bothered about the treasure which her husband had accumulated over the years. There were all signs of dejection and dread on her face. In fact, her whole body was trembling. I read her heart too. It was frightened of the consequences. Already as I understood it later, her husband was tied and with the effect of medicine he was made unconscious.

Nothing worried the children. They continued sleeping. No neighbour, however, dared to come there. Thereafter, three more robbers got in and opened the treasures. They pocketed Rs. 52,000 which was black money Swaminathan as the Controller of Examination of Pampapati University had gathered, eighty-five grams of gold most of which was presented to his wife in consideration of his favours, and some pearls, diamonds, precious articles and rich sarees which had cost them not less than Rs. 29,000. Neither they spoke nor made any noise. Everything went on as though a detective film. Swaminathan was unconscious his face cast downward, while his beautiful dame unfortunately defenceless lay beside me like a subdued deer. However, to start with, the robbers did not notice me. Some of them, in fact, strictly guarded the event. Now and then certain code-like sounds were heard and unheard but I could not perceive any of their meaning. I was simply consoling the fallen angel.

'Don't worry madam. They seem to be a gang of great decoits and it's very difficult to face them,' I told her. But she could not talk to me. Anyway, this did not hinder my monologue. Good she nodded to my consolations.

'What matters most is your life. And you're lucky that they've not seduced you,' I told her honestly. Occasional were her sighs. She showed her hands which were tightened by strings. Subsequently with my kitchen knife I took no time to liberate this Sita Then I gave her my *lungi* with which she began to cover her body. This time too I could not help looking at her. However, I did not see her with any bestial passions.

When robbers looted every precious thing including money, one of them came to my room. I do not know whether he came to see her or me. Mostly as I guessed it, he came indoors to take a glance at her ravishing body. I thought it was the same person who had dropped her there before. Besides, another reason for his coming into my room was that I had made some noise.

He came in suddenly but made no noise. His attention was at her nudity alone. Unfortunately sudden was his kissing her which apparently enraged me. So promptly I rose up to the situation and avoided him while he was likely to embrace her. It was like playing her husband's role there. Rukmini too directly turned to me for protection. Thereafter, I pulled his hands but he threw me away quite powerfully. Immediately I asked her to get in another room and I screamed loudly. Consequently two more rascals rushed there. Now the event took a drastic turn. One of them at once kicked me for treasures. He spoke in erratic Kannada and I could not understand him. Quickly on their demand, I could not help giving them Rs. 500 which was my only pocket money. Soon they took away my golden coloured wristwatch, which had cost me not less than Rs. 900. Thinking further search futile, the taller one of them kicked me once again. A great kick in bone. Since it was a time for their departure, without troubling any of us, they decamped the spot hurriedly. But before they could go away, the particular robber who tried to embrace Rukmini gave me another bold kick, while his colleague burst into a peel of laughter.

I uttered but no words. Great was the kick I had received. The pain in my bony body had already begun. However, I wasted no time. I opened the inside door, which disconnected me from Swaminathan and his family. Finally, I went in courageously and threw her a nighty.

'Come in madam. Take your saree if you want,' I told her shyly.

'Thank you,' she made a feeble reply.

Thereafter, I saw Swaminathan lying there as if defunct. When I checked his pulse, I found him still alive. But because of the impact of certain chemicals, he could not talk to me for some time. Nor did he look like us there. The children remained yet undisturbed, while the landlady turned busy in verifying the things looted.

'Madam take this golden ring,' I told her in a soothing voice. I gave her all the important items that had lain there because of robber's negligence. But I could not open the doors of house which were bolted from cutside to avoid our disturbance. Then I put a zero bulb into Swaminathan's hall as the miscreants had destroyed all lights. Indeed, they had looted things amazingly just with torches. Broken pieces of bulbs, door, glasses, boxes and the like were ample on the marble flooring. I also helped the woman in tidying up the house. However the house looked fine from outside, its beauty and serenity had disappeared. Besides, Rukmini was awstruck to see her husband still fast sleeping. But I took no time to console and convince her about the chemical blow.

No sooner I consoled her than he gained his consciousness. He got up. But he was shocked by my presence. He had risen like a newlyborn. This scene was very akin to Satyavahan's mythological reawakening by Savitri's prayer to the All Merciful. The time I narrated him the tale, he began to recollect things. Fortunately he did not worry much about his treasure that was lifted. Nor did he remember the fact that his wife was barebodied when she slept and something happened to her. Luckily this was in the dame's favour. I too had told her that she should not tell her husband anything about the robber's mischief, or of my seeing her. Great was her thankfulness to me both for my counsel and broadmindedness. She also requested me never to make a move to destroy her image or affect her feminine grace. After I consoled them, I went to my room and slept for a while. But great was the ache in my bones!

When it was five o' clock dawn, somebody opened the doors

of Swaminathan's house. Thereafter Swaminathan opened the door of my room. At once, like a curious child, I rushed outside. Still there was much dark as it was a Sabbath. But men and women had already gathered there in a large number. When I made an observation of the phenomenon, I was to admire the decoits' skills. Meanwhile, one after another, many police vehicles rushed to the spot. So the dark began to disappear.

People spoke and their talks were noisy. One said, 'robbers looted many houses in Ramanagar,' while others said they were terrible in appearance. The man in black rags told the crowd that he had really seen them at 4.30 am while he got down from his roof. People whose houses were looted burst into wild tears and sobs and womenfolk cried and wept since they had lost their valuables. Gangamma was one of them and she wept very bitterly. This drew the undivided attention of the crowd. Ramkrishna said they took away his taperecorder, which he had kept for identifying their sounds. Virabhadra abusing the robbers in vulgar terms spoke of his depression. Many people spoke many things. Some of them enlisted the items that were looted from five houses including Swaminathan's. A man who heard these things took no time to calculate their value but his calculation did not include all of Swaminathan's treasure. As Swaminathans had a superior complexity, now they did not come out from their cell. Soon the Secretary of Ramanagar Welfare Association hurried over there to look into the details. It was he who had rung up the police first. At once an SP and his subordinates rushed to the spot. When the Secretary chided the SP about the negligence of police in maintaining law and order in suburbia, the officer could not avoid him. But he was shrewd enough to acknowledge the ineffectiveness of police and to blame political leaders who used to encourage such things. But Virabhadra accused the SP of mistakes police committed daily. He said, 'police never come to the rescue of common people. 'They come only at the end of problems,' he added it ironically. His friend Ramakrishna, who had lost articles worth Rs. 15,000, supported him throughout the wrangle.

'What's the use of accusations?' the SP asked Virabhadra displaying his sympathy for him. This angered Ramakrishna.

'It's done because you're not patrolling the extension areas. Your people have become lazy and always they are in league with criminals,' he retorted. In fact, he lost his temper. The bystanders shared his sorrow and admired his brilliance in pleading.

'See Ramakrishna I admit some of your views that a few police might have become lazy. But I don't think they are in league with criminals,' the SP spoke to defend the honour of his department.

Then the secretary of the area lodged a written complaint. He asked the SP to detect the robbers and do justice to the unfortunate residents. Then onwards people in large number visited the spot and police controlled them. The robbery was published in all the next day newspapers. Consequently with the help of residents, the police patrolling was seriously begun.

Be it as it may I made my private inspection of the treasures looted. The robbers had taken away Rs. 1,58,000 in cash and valuables worth Rs. 85,000. Swaminathan alone had lost a wealth of Rs. 75,000 and though the loss of mine was just a thousand and above, it greatly affected my daily life.

ooo

8

ENCOUNTER WITH A SPIRIT

IT WAS a festival day. Both myself and my friend Chanagouda desired to go to his mango grove to bring some green mangoes for chatny as well as for eating. Soon he suggested me that we should go there early, otherwise, he felt, the climate would upset us.

'D'you think it can trouble us greatly?' I asked him to know whether he had possessed any meteorological knowledge.

'Yea, certainly. Therefore, let's go soon. Besides, you know how the place where now we're going is a dangerous one,' said Chanagouda. He was right though I did not realise it. Then we began our journey a mile away from the village of Telsang towards east. Indeed, on the way we saw the front house Gangi, a beautiful callgirl who resided at a house near Lakkavva temple's tanners' colony. Then my nose scratching brother came on the way and asked us to return home soon. With him was his bad friend Kenchappa. Both were homeward bound. Meanwhile as we were young and immature, soon we fell in revelry. Admittedly Chanagouda was a very sensuous boy of twenty-five. He began to talk of Gangi whom daily he would meet at his field.

Obviously familiar with cathouse business, Chanagouda, a loose morale friend of mine had been with Gangi manytimes merry-making. Even her ignorant fat mother allowed her without knowing the worst consequences. So like his father Chanagouda frequented the women who lifted their legs. He was very clever in enticing dames who were ignorant but sexy enough to succumb. Usually he carried this business at his farm. As his politically known grandfather was buried there and his spirit witchhaunted many people, nobody dared to cross their heath. This deathly silence helped his business flourish.

We went on thinking about the right and wrong of extra-marital and homo-sexual matters. At the end of our journey, we found his fertile mango grove and maize crop. Beautiful was the crop — almost ready for harvesting.

'D'you know what happened to my strong uncle Shivaraj when he met a police officer yesterday?' asked Chanagouda to change the tone of our talk.

'What happened?'

'See, my uncle went to the police station and informed the PSI not to meddle into the details of murder case in which my father was involved. But when the latter did not obey him, my strong uncle threatened him,' Chanagouda stopped for breathforce.

'Then what happened?' asked I.

'Can't you guess? He left the case and ran off. He didn't question my father further as he was afraid of us,' said Chanagouda adjusting a cigar in his stinking mouth. To him pride of power came by birth as his great ancesters had ruled the village as Patels. These Patels were known for their filth and dirty business in the village and often they complicated the village politics solely for crushing their enemies.

'D'you like to drink?' presently Chanagouda asked me.

'No; that won't suit to my health,' I tried my best to avoid his enticement.

'You're a simpleton. Don't worry. I'll teach you smoking and drinking. They're good for health,' said he. Admittedly he went on encouraging me to learn them. Also he assured that I need not bother about buying them. Anyway drinks and cigars were available to him by those who were afraid of his gaffer's ghost. People gave them to his family just to please the gluttonous spirit. Consequently Chanagouda and his hundred kindreds freely enjoyed such things.

'Friend drinking is very good for health. So try to take

kundry,' he said the next moment. By kundry he meant bottles. I was familiar with people who drank kundries and I had already got a fair idea about it. But as I was under the sway of Gandhi I hated both smoking and drinking. However, when I said him about Gandhi's opposition to such drowsiness producing things, Chanagouda criticised Gandhi invidiously. He said, 'it's Gandhi who made harizans and higher castes equal. Though he brought independence to India, he led to the partition of country,' said he proding his long fingers.

Chanagouda loved Acharya Rajanish most. In the beginning I was unaware of Rajanish and his ideals. Only when Chanagouda made it clear that Rajanish advocated the habits he followed for a healthy life, I realised that Rajanish should have been the largest version of this filth loving Chanagouda.

The field came. So we stood there amidst his mango grove. Then Chanagouda said 'we'd get mangoes both for chatny and eating.' Meanwhile I suggested him the biggest tree that bore very good fruits. But he took to an old tree which his grandfather Rudragouda had planted. His mausoleum existed thereunder. Along the old relic already a bottle of kundry and many other items of eating, drinking and smoking had been kept by those whom the dead had tormented. Although I advised Chanagouda not to drink wine, he drank all the full bottle.

'D'you know how I like cigars?' he burst in laughter. I simply neglected it. Though unafraid of his usual cries, I advised him not to eat the boiled eggs which, like flowers before an idol, were lain beside the tomb.

'No, we'd eat them. You don't know how you can get power by this,' he smiled upon me. Then he eat four eggs and gave me the remaining two. Although I was afraid of eating any of them, my hunger compelled me.

'Chanagouda if you want, drink the cococola,' told I pointing to him another drink.

No doubt, soon he drank it.

Then there was a deep silence.

There were *beedis* too. He took two of them. So in all, Chanagouda drank a bottle of Kundry, ate four boiled eggs, smoked two *beedis* and like one possessed he spoke for an hour. I knew whenever he drank he fell in a heavy talk. No doubt, he could talk like a summer ghost. But in reality, I was never afraid of such things since I knew him closely. Presently we were engrossed there. Even no woodcutters who busied at a near distance looked at our foolhardiness.

'Now will you climb up the tree to get fruits?' asked I.

'How many fruits do you want?' he asked me in turn, blowing up a big cloud of smoke.

'Just five-six,' I replied timidly.

'Okay to you five-six and to me ten-twenty,' he spoke feebly.

'Why you take more?' I tried to trace a mystery.

'Because my lover Ningi wants some of them,' said he happily climbing up the tree. During the next ten minutes, he threw down more than twenty-five mangoes. Every one of them like tiny coconuts could be seen on the earth. I collected them as eagerly as I listened to the tune of his lyric. We went on doing this. But the time he finished a song on his old lover, at once he underwent a great tremor in his physical and mental posture. Suddenly he sat on a twig of the tree cross-legged and like a man possessed, burst out.

'O! Come here,' he screamed at the top of his voice. Indeed, presently I was between a deep and devil. Afraid of the whole situation, I took to my heels. But his voice obsessed me like anything and he threatened me to obey.

Rudragouda's ghost stopped me running away.

'O! Son of mine come here,' he ordered. 'Don't worry I won't harm you. Like Chanagouda, you're dear to me. Come on. Why do you fly and do a futile effort to save your skin. Come here.'

'I'm coming,' I replied him trembling.

'Are you scared of me. Get here. You're not in good terms with your brother, why?' he stopped to clear his throat.

Though Chanagouda never spoke to me in this vein, his grandfather's spirit, whenever came, retorted me giving advice. Even, this was in my interest. Now sat cross-leged in the tree, which he had planted in 1910, while he had been the village Patel under the British, he began lecturing me.

'See these days your friend Chanagouda has become a bad boy. I wonder whether he improves. He drinks, smokes, plays and does anything that's extraneous to the boys of your age. If he goes on like this, one day he'll go to dogs. Won't you think so? Are you there or not?' he asked me to know whether or not I was listening to him.

'O!...I'm here...I'm collecting fruits,' I told him frightened though I did not do what I meantby.

'O!...Damn it...Stop it I say...Listen to me,' thundered he in a leonine voice.

'Yes...Yes...' I nodded my head in perfect obedience.

'Hm! As I know even he frequents brothels. Tell him he should stop it. Also tell him he should not drink. Nor should he smoke either? Also tell him he'd study hard. Also tell him, like me, he'd become a great man. Understand this?' he came down heavily. Already his voice had lost its vigour.

'Yes, yes.'

However, I could not catch some of his 'alsos', I simply gave him my attention. In fact, I went on yessing, while he kept on alsoing. Afraid of his demoniac fury, cross-leged posture on the tree and his leonine voice, no surprise I had already urinated in my halfpant. Had he threatened me futher, I would have even defacated there. Thank God. Luckily that did not happen.

After a good deal of smoking, the ghost went off to much of my best relief.

So after the exhaution of inner fury, the avaricious spirit of grandsignor Rudragouda, from the earthen body of my hundred and eight habits friend Chanagouda vanished. It was fortunate that the boy in the tree did not fall down. Mostly the eggs and drinks he had before supported him. Proir to this event, I had heard people talking about ghosts, which according to them, ate anything and stayed at graveyards. Ghosts, I had heard, could work miracles. They were afraid of nothing. But so far I did not see any of them. Accordingly, I did not believe them. Then another idea that my ten years back died mother had said quickly entered my fragile sensibility. After understanding this possession, ghosts, I thought, would be nothing but this kind of spirits. At this time what once my long haired brother said came to my senile memory. I recollected ghosts were afraid of fire and water. Even my uncle's advice that when we encounter a ghost, we should throw fire over them came to my broken mind. This would make them fly away. However, what I just saw was not this kind of ghost. Nor was I a ghost girl rider? Still the pictures of ghosts that were very big, very tall, very dark like those of Thomas Hardy's description of them in his elegies disturbed me. The fierceness of ghosts awstruck my mind. Even I knew nothing about what I should do then.

'O! Friend what're you doing?' soon Chanagouda himself broke the heavy silence.

I could not reply him at once.

Silence still reigned there.

'How many fruits are there? Have you counted them?' he returned to the original idea of our fruitgathering.

'O!..P..l..e..a..s..e..come down,' I said him subdueing my fear. I was gathering my courage. Though we needed some more fruits as per our earlier calculation, now I did not mind it. My immediate concern was to fly home at the earliest. Meanwhile Chanagouda having been strained badly could not alight as quickly as he climbed it up. So when he tried to come down, I lent him my benigh hand and he came down safe.

'I'm very tired. I can't understand why. Whenever I climb up my grandfather's tree, I'll be fatigued a great deal,' Chanagouda broke thus. His right hand was on his head. Presently he could not walk any distance. Rudragouda's holding had sapped him. As his stock of knowledge went, because of this only people respected him as much as they respected Rudragouda decades ago. Why not for this reason only? The dead politician came in him when there fell a necessity of chiding anybody. The things he could ask included many edible items. As a result, when people passed by his grave, he used to frighten them — for things like — banana, eggs, cigars, lemons, coconuts, sometimes hens. But nobody knew his kindred ate them instead. Everyone had the vista that at midnight Rudragouda'a ghost could materialise itself into a human form and enjoy the items fondly. Hence, none crossed the adjoining crossroad during any of the dark hours. Even people avoided it at dawn or dusk. Only the old woman Mrs. Venkavva would pass by his tomb at the approach of dark. Since she had been his kept and had no fear of him as such, she dared to pass there. But this notorious damsal had passed away ten years ago at the age of 110. Anyway people who heard Rudragouda's tale used to tell their children about him just to keep them on string. They told their kids they would be taken to Rudragouda's phantom if they did not read their English lessons.

Now Chanagouda trotted beside me. It was already pitch dark. However, we managed to get a nearby going bullock cart that belonged to my neighbour, the meat eating Parappa. On my request Parappa took the cart first to Chanagouda's house through the village rustic streets. Deliberately on the way neither Chanagouda nor I spoke to each other. He had slept on my laps and I had been mostly silent. We were forced by the situation not to indulge in any colloquy. Only I told Parappa that Chanagouda was not well in reply to one of his many troubling questions. When Rudragouda's house came near, we safely stopped the convey. Soon his father took him home. Subsequently, for the next two weeks or so, thank heaven, I did not know what happened to me or to Chanagouda.

Thereafter, like a school dropout at once I hurried home. My nose-scratching brother scolded me to have arrived home late. My eldest brother would inquire me affectionately. But he was out of the station. After some handfuls of evening meal, I went to bed complaining severly against myself. For the next three days, I did not know what happened to me, for I was badly ill as something strained me substantially. Many people came to my big house to see me. Meantime frivolous rumours about my ill health spread like wildfire. Different people spoke differently. After three deadly days passed, I became rather wakeful and I could understand the externals. Already the news that a phantom shook me was lively spread in the townlet. People who believed in Rudragouda's ghost talked that the ghost came into my body as it came to Changouda's the other day. But none had talked this more vividly than my backbiting aunt Bouravva. She did not like me. There was always an air of uneasiness between us. So she hated me like anything and she did whatever she could to spoil my image. She spread the matter to the fronthouse Suvarna and to the back door house Kasibai. She also said it to my old gossip loving teacher Sharada. Sharada said this to her story loving sister Sakubai. Shobha, Sakubai's daughter who was my classmate and interested in me, heard this with demoniac curiosity. Sometimes, Sharada, Sakubai and Shobha — all S's sat together and gossiped. I was, they felt, really punished by god to have disobeyed my teacher once in my fifth standard. This was an old incident. A bizarre one. Radha, Shobha's friend listened to it and took it to the whole Shepherds Alley. Thus my illness became a grass for those who knew me and interested in knowing about Rudragouda, the doyan of my village ghosts.

Meanwhile I came to know that my nose-scratching brother had heretofore put to the ghost Rudragouda his favourite things. When I recovered, he told me, he had kept there one coconut, one bottle of wine, two pockets of fine cigars, three boiled eggs, four lemons and five tandori breads. So after putting these — one, two, three, four, fives — how can he forget to console me that I really got some recovery. Being an orphan boy, since at the age of ten I had lost my parents — I could not tell my sorrow to anyone but to this Chanagouda. O! Now everything was changed. Further people advised me to avoid this marvellous boy. So going again to his field was something I could not think of. Not only

I most of those who experienced Rudragouda's trepidation scarcely went there. When somebody spoke of this bloody Gouda's vagaries, people shuddered inwardly. What ghosts could mean was also studied by a B.Sc. student in my neighbourhood. Some college students who were shortly to go to Pampapati University discussed about ghosts hotly. Many of them said ghosts do not exist. But none of them dared to go to Rudragouda's mango grove. This made me think ghosts do exist inasmuch as this was amusingly reasonable. Though they did not believe in ghosts, they did not like to go to that Egdon like vast tract of land. When they were enquired about this, they simply dodged me saying that they disliked the heath. But in truth, like us, these shrinking fellows were frightened of the Witch of Vendor.

When I fully recovered, my diurnal activities began again. But people kept on enquiring me. Those who knew the event personally talked themselves. The ghostal Gouda, people regretted, even did not spare me, a boy and his grandson's close friend. But nobody, as I came to know it later, knew the reality. Verily the spirit did not haunt me. In fact, Rudragouda loved me as he loved Chanagouda. Only I was afraid of that deathly appearance and that alone made me ill. Really by this time nobody knew Rudragouda better than myself, not even Chanagouda in whom he survived at times. What a rare happening? I conversed with a man who ruled the village for more than fifty years and commanded the respect of Englishmen. I spoke with him as I spoke with his grandson. No matter I suffered, I was proud of the event. I saw the absorbing personality of the 19th century born man who died only in the mid 20th century only after India attained independence. Like Thomas Hardy who met the old prisoners of Napolionic wars and was very glad about the event while he wrote the epic drama *The Dynasts,* I amused myself over the spectacular phenomenon. It is a matter of self-satisfaction when one can see the friend of his great ancestor. After all this Gouda was an intimate friend of money-loving Huchchappa, my grand-father. However, I could not ask this Gouda about my grandshire as I was simply upset by his pallid appearance. But I got a fair view of the 19th century gentleman.

Believe it or not, still people continued to see me with an air of interest. Owing to this event, bodily I was greatly weakened. This added a greater charm to the colourful happening. Those who heard much about ghosts and me spoke that the dead disturbed me. Indeed, people looked at me interestedly as they did at Diana who died in a car crash recently because of photo taking people's chase. However, children were afraid of me whenever they saw me on the way, at bus stand or beside an alehouse. They never dared to talk to me. Nor did they jeer at me either? Most of them were frightened of me thinking that I might enter into their bodies. In fact, many people considered me an obsolete.

Thus, passed the days. When I became fairly well, one day my grandmother who lived still though aged 105, came to me with a great care. Obviously she sat beside me consoling.

'Don't go my child that way again,' her tongue shivered.

'Yes,' I nodded meekly.

'What Rudragouda told you?' she asked with difficulty. She was very curious to know about one of her contemporaneous persons who had shone in the sphere of village politics.

'He asked me to be good and do good,' said I smiling.

'A good advice…,' she smiled upon me gazing at those who sat beside her.

'He advised me to work hard for coming up in life,' I went on

'This's still a very nice word. What matters most in life,' my grandmother continued 'is work. Man is nothing but a sum of his works.' Then she said, 'unless you work hard, you can't shine in society,' while before she could retire to her bed she echoed Basavanna 'WORK IS WORSHIP.'

❍❍❍

9
RAMU'S CONVERSATION WITH HIS DEAD MOTHER

ONE DAY when Ramu was sitting in the backyard of his house, somebody hastened there calling him loudly.

'What's the matter?' Ramu asked.

'Y…o…u…r…mo…the…r…'s come here,' the other stammered hysterically.

'What…What d'you mean?' Ramu asked him frightened. There was a sense of dread and wonder in his shivering. All knew his mother had died a long ago. She had expired two decades back after the death of his father in a gruesome lorry accident. So she could not survive her husband for any length of time. She died young and unhappy. Ramu's mother, people felt, suffered badly. Added to her husband's sad demise, a deadly cancer had quickened her departure in a hastening manner.

Wonderful enough Shankrappa told Ramu that his mother had come. This shocked Ramu aged twenty-one. He could not believe it. He was at a loss to understand the matter. Many thoughts boldly gripped him. In fact, he could not believe his mother's arrival to the living world. He thought again whether a defunct woman could come back to life. Of course, she may be his mother, how can a dead woman turn up alive? This disturbed him. Even whether her ghost might have come there occurred to his immature mind. Anyway it was quite riddlesome, unbelievable, unthinkable — absurd. Besides, he was afraid of meeting her. He dreaded whether she could take him away. Still ideas of ghosts came confusing. More he recollected the stories of ghosts, more timorous he turned. His fear was strengthened. However, Ramu sat up for a while only to be called by Shankrappa once more to see his mother in the inner room of their house where many a kindred had already gathered.

On his coming indoors Ramu saw Somu, his eldest brother sitting beside Chandramma, his youngest aunt. Many more persons including Ramnath, Shankrappa, Surappa, Danamma, — his relatives had gathered there earnest. His sister Kalpana sat there aside the woman who was talking like one possessed. Really she possessed. This woman was Chandramma, the wife of Surappa who was the youngest brother of Ramu's father. Earlier nobody knew the fact that Renuka, Ramu's mother would come in Chandramma's body. This was called spirit-occupation which but frightened everyone. Therefore all there had sat silent. Even the children created no noise. They were afraid of the ghostly presence. Undoubtedly most of the elders did not dare to talk dismayed of Renuka's holding. But Surappa engaged the woman boldly. They sat quite next to her. Meanwhile Ramu squatted in a corner not far away. He wanted not to be chided by his mother. So now his mother could not notice him.

'Why has he encroached our land?' pointing to Shankrappa, Renuka, the dead mother, now in a high spirit questioned him. It meant that Basappa, the adamant brother of Ramu's father had encroached an acre of Somu's land which annoyed the dead woman. That is why she had made her hideous presence felt there today.

'Who you mean?' Surappa asked her dryly. He did not catch her point easily.

'Basappa...Basappa,' cried the woman fretfully. She was impatient. Her sound was terrific. Whenever Somu, Ramu, Bhimu and Kalpana were troubled by others, she used to come in Chandramma's body and chide the culprits. On this occasion, she came to enquire about the encroachment of her land by Basappa, the audacious neighbourhood relative.

'Yes, yes, he's encroached some of your land,' Surappa

interrupted to reduce her acidity as it was in his wife's body the spirit had come. He thought if she turned vehement, it could seriously affect Chandramma's health. Hence, Surappa saved no efforts in pacifying the witch. He wondered whether the sorcerer might frequently possess his wife. But he could not tell it as it would hurt Renuka's sons.

'I know why Basappa's done it?' she screamed loudly and with her hands she produced sounds alarming. The fury she created terrified all the timid around. Meanwhile on her mother's suggestion Somu called Basappa to her presence. So that, he felt, she could easily settle the contentious issue, which he could not do during the past three years. Ramu sat alert to see whether their land dispute would be resolved. When Basappa did not turn up, on Surappa's advice, a boy was dispatched for him again. Consequently Basappa came there but he did not know that this witch had come. Had he known it, he would have taken to his heels.

'Why you've encroached an acre of our land?' the woman interrogated the newcomer. Awe-struck by this, Basappa did not reply her at once. Almost he sat down dumb-founded. O! He sat down trembling.

'I asked you Basappa as to why you've encroached my land?' repeated Renuka in Chandramma's voice. Almost a thunderbolt with lightening. This time with an increased vigour.

'Because…it…it…belong…s…to…me,' the wicked man stammered.

'How does it belong to you. Can you explain me?'

'It simply belongs to me.'

'Then why you didn't get it when we'd been alive?' Renuka argued vehemently. She was furious. She was right. So for a minute or two, Basappa lost his heart and sat down terror-struck. He felt he could not justify his stand.

'Give your reasons brother,' Surappa poked his nose.

'See I couldn't claim it by the time you're alive,' Basappa

spoke faintly. Really the words on his lips failed to make any sense.

'That's what I'm asking you… Why you didn't do it then? Were you scared of us? Or have you done it now, as my sons are not strong enough to overpower you? D'you want to disturb them…. If so why?' an array of questions followed.

'Now I can't answer you,' Basappa tried to dodge her.

'Are you afraid of me? A nonsense bully…Tell me what's your ulterior motive behind this…D'you think your sons are destined to enjoy the ill-gotten property?…Suppose you don't give it back, I'll witchhaunt your family…Remember…'she scolded him pauselessly. She did not need even any breathforce. This astonished the gathered. The children were overawed. This amused those who hated Basappa inwardly. But none save Somu and Surappa dared to meddle in the matter.

'Basappa make your stand clear lest you will incur her wrath further,' said Shankrappa honestly.

'Now I can't make it clear.'

'Why?'

'I've to think over it,' he held the ground.

'Then why didn't you think about the consequence while you usurped our land?' Somu cut it terribly. Now in his mother's presence, he was strong to counterargue.

'Because it belonged to me.'

'Then answer her,' Somu jeopardised him. Also Basappa's stubbornness hurt everyone. Having impatiently listened to his unsatisfactory grunting, Renuka grew stronger.

'See Basappa you'd give up the land within a month or two. Otherwise, I'll disturb your lineage. Bear it in mind that if my righteous children are troubled, I come to their rescue again. May be I may come here anytime. If you don't yield to them I'll spoil your family happiness until you're made to accept their terms. As you protect the interests of your sons, I've to protect the interests of my sons, shouldn't I Surappa?' she turned to the nearer one for support.

'I don't think it's wrong,' the middle-aged man broke noddingly.

'I'm one with you mother,' Ramu said.

'Why should he upset us unnecessarily,' Somu burst.

This embarrassed Basappa. As he did not justify his stand, he incurred the wrath of many persons. He learnt the people there abhored him, while the children looked at him reproachfully. Occasional was everyone's persuasion yet. It was when none was kind towards him including Surappa, Basappa assuring the spirit some settlement decided to disappear.

'Remember what I've told you today. If you delay, I'll trouble you like anything. Understand it?' Renuka shot boldly. 'And it's left to you whether to recourse to reconciliation or to incur my further frenzy. In case you don't change your mind you'll have to suffer.'

However without returning her any reply, Basappa, a den of villainy swiftly left for his home. Now he was on the verge of sobbing. Had he been a woman, he would have burst out weeping. Unfortunately that did not happen.

Thereupon like the Ganga of rainy season, the tide of events turned. Renuka gazed at others her voice becoming mellow. She saw the condition of her children. She smiled upon all those sat around there.

'How're you Ramu? Are you studying well?' asked she.

'I'm well. This year I'm in X standard,' replied the only educated boy. Now he was bold enough to talk to her.

'How d'you do?' he asked her.

'I'm well.' Affectionate was her reply.

'Where're you living mother?' Ramu enquired her. This looked serious to others as they did not anticipate it.

'Now I'm living in our field and whenever you're troubled, I gladly come down here to guide you. Are you happy Kalpana, my dear girl? How are you at school?' she spoke gently. Indeed, she looked a matron.

'I'm doing well mother,' Kalpana said.

It is because of the private talk, all the children gathered there were made to go away. Now the two sons, a daughter and Surappa remained there undisturbed.

'Where's our father now?' asked Ramu.

'He's already gone to heaven,' said she proudly.

'Then why are you still in the wind?' asked he.

'Yes, I'm still in the wind, as I died unsatisfied at an age when I had yet to enjoy life. Therefore, I've not yet achieved a level of self-satisfaction. So until I get it, I'll have to wander here and there. You know how persons of undersatisfaction live a miserable life. Mine is a similar case,' spoke she abruptly.

'D'you have any friends with you?' the boy put it plainly. As she went on replying them, Ramu, like a child questioning its mother, began examining her about the mystery of underworld. Since he was aware of the wonderful power of spirits, he decided to know the unknown. He was fascinated by the unfamiliar. But Somu, the eldest did not wish to ask her anything about the invisible. His immediate concern was only to get her moral support. But Ramu's concern was beyond that. He was interested in probing the remote corners of life. He was busy in enquiring his mother about the nature and condition of nether world, while Kalpana took no interest in any of these.

'How is the world you live in mother?' Ramu broke curiously.

'See, the world I live in is full of dazzling spirits. People who've died prematurely still live with me. Unlike the living, we live without any food or shelter. Like a huge prison house, ours is a mixed world where co-spirits disturb none. There we're all equal. Ours's a total democracy. Admittedly we're free from family worries, worldly fetters and the like. Even we need not think of our food. God's asked us to remain in this mode until our sins're washed away or forgotten. For some years, we've to suffer, wander and warble away our time. He's also warned us not to disturb you, the bodily folk and the lucky people. Only when there is a great necessity of mine to you I come over here. No matter, how the people object to it, I don't care,' Renuka stopped her monologue.

'Who're there with you?' both Ramu and Kalpana asked her together. So the woman could not understand either.

'Talk one by one,' said she comically.

'Who're with you?' this time Ramu alone asked.

'There're, indeed, many persons with me. Both male and female, Hindu and Muslim, even Christian. The good and bad, the haves and have-nots — all together. My friend Sridevi is with me. So are Sudha and her husband who murdered each other. But when I went to this windworld, I'd not get your father. Thank God. He's already joined the rank of immortals.'

'Does Sridevi, like you, come down?'.

'No, she doesn't.'

'Why?'

'Because she died aged. Since her passions were spent, she didn't like to meet her kith. Nor is it necessary for her? I too couldn't come here in case Basappa didn't torture you,' the benign mother spoke over her earthly mission.

'Would you take me with you mother?' Kalpana asked her innocently.

'No; none of you should come to my world as you're yet to enjoy your life until Yama invites you.'

'That's true,' Surappa supported her. Presently his smoking disturbed her. But it seems none noticed it.

'See my girl everyone should lead a happy life. And in no state of affairs you'd aspire to escape the hectic activities of life — good or evil or middling. Anyway since we're mortals, one day or other, all of you've to retire from the world,' spoke she a universal truth.

Admittedly Surappa nodded and Somu joined him. There was a pause. None dared to ask her as to why man fell from God's grace. They simply admired the beauty of her veiled and unfathomable journey from the airy world to the world of living and loving beings.

'Would you like to come here again? Ramu dashed a question.

'If you land into troubles.'

This question gave a room for some doubting. Then with an affectionate grace, Renuka desired to know whether any of them liked her coming there.

'D'you want me appear here.'

'Yes, we like your presence,' said some reluctantly.

But none was sure of it.

'However, you don't like us, d'you?' she interrogated them. She felt hurt.

'Sometimes that's true,' Surappa said her being afraid of his dame's health.

'Don't worry. I won't frequent you,' Renuka said him. Her tone was assuring.

'That's alright. But the children are scared of you,' Surappa muttered.

'D'you want anything to eat,' Ramu asked her sympathetically.

'No; I don't trouble you. If you live happily, I'm glad enough not to come here,' the possessed woman sobbed.

'Alright don't worry about it,' said Ramu more to himself.

'Well. Now I'd like to drive your attention to me,' in a huff began she. 'Don't quarrel. Please live happily.' The flow of her thoughts continued. But not half an hour later than this she felt the worldings around her were bored of her. So she decided to retire to her atmospheric world. Subsequently, Chandramma in whose body Renuka had descended down shuddered continuously. The time the transition was over, Chandramma became the original Chandramma — a dark eyed middle-aged woman.

ooo

10

A MAN WITH A WRITER ONE EVENING

RAYANNA WAS a poet. Already he had five collections of poems and short stories to his credit. 'An Old Wine In A New Bottle' was one of his books that brought him fortunes. He was a voracious reader. He read for twelve hours a day and wrote for three hours regularly. His memory was striking. Whatever he read a year ago or two, he could recollect it with ease and grace. What many people could not do at his age, he had accomplished it brilliantly. A mere M.A. graduate in History, who failed to do an M. Phil or Ph.D., because of financial sieve, he turned to poetry writing — his first love. Although he did not study language, he possessed an inborn talent for versification and story telling. Many people knew much about him though not personally. Several functions in which he had participated brought him a name. He was, indeed, respected in the literary circles. Even he was frequently invited as a guest to functions in Pampapati University. Everyone who read him apprised his talent sincerely. In fact, reading public encouraged him. No wonder, he was a loveable person in Omnagar, Pampapattan.

It was an April Sunday. In part due to lord's day, there was devil-dark everywhere. The tiny house wherein Rayanna lived was a room of a big building. It belonged to Kenchayya, a Revenue Officer of Pampapattan. Like Shivagiri, the nearest suburb, the locality was densely populated. But Kenchayya's house stood in a corner of far-flung buildings. Because of his corrupt way of life, Kenchayya had earned a lot. But most of his acquisition was invested in his palatial building. A portion of the house was rented to Rayanna.

The same day when the sun fell, Kenchayya came out and his eyes fell on Rayanna, who was sitting there reading Milton.

'O! you're reading.'

'Yes, uncle,' came a humble reply.

'Well...'

'May I know what you're reading?'

'John Milton, an English poet of 17th century.'

Kenchayya remembered his reading of Milton's 'On His Blindness' way back in those days when he studied for matriculation. However, in regard to English literature, specially English fiction, he had been obsessed with one general conviction that it dealt with woman, love and sex. Or as he thought it, it was more on sex than on anything. Promptly he desired to know it in a great length.

'Shall I think that woman and sex is the main theme of English literature?'

'No; it can't be said like that. All other aspects of life are portrayed in English literature. For example, if you take English poetry or fiction, nature, human activities, religion, love, woman are the themes. But sometimes, as you feel, love is major there. For instance, Lawrence's novels.'

'Yes; I know Lawrence's novels are sexy,' improving his position on a nearby platform, Kenchayya desired to know more of this.

'Have you ever read his *Sons and Lovers*?'

'Yes,' replied the other.

'Then...can you narrate me its story?'

'Alright,' Rayanna began, 'see in that novel Lawrence writes about a family. The master of the house has his wife very fair. So are his sons especially the eldest one. The master is a collier. His wife, like yours, is a housewife — good. But her carnal passions are turbulent. Since her husband works in a distant place, he can't be about the home always. Consequently, she develops an affair with her eldest son. No doubt, he too is handsome and loveable. So over the years, a kind of love sprouts between the two. She asks him to satisfy her itch, while unaware of his position, he submits. Thus, the story develops vividly,' said Rayanna earnestly. No doubt, Kenchayya had forgotten the whole world, while the other was engrossed in telling him the momentous account.

'So in all, you mean a mother sleeps with her son, doesn't she?' Kenchayya asked the younger to confirm the heresy.

'Certainly.'

'But don't you think it's disgusting?'

'Of course! But …Many times this kind of libidinous things happen to be the main theme of some writers…You know Sex Appeal is the Greatest.'

'Is it the theme of his other novels too?' the older asked.

'Yes…but they differ in details. However, his other novels *Lady Chatterlay's Lover* and *The Rainbow* deal with similar themes.'

'What about Hardy?'

'You mean Thomas Hardy?' shot the younger.

'Yea'.

'See; in some of Hardy's novels, we come across interpersonal relationships such as a man falling in love with his cousin, broken off weddings, divorce cases and illicit affairs. In fact, Hardy writes about men and women, who marry in haste and repent at leisure,' Rayanna stopped for a breathforce.

'O!…O!…O!…I think events such as mother falling in love with her son are more interesting,' being interested in the charms of sex, Kenchayya returned to the old theme.

'That's true.'

'Why this kind of illaffairs take place?'

'See as my knowledge goes all kinds of sexual relationships have taken place. You know there're homosexual things as well.

Man because of his lust or ignorance doesn't hesitate to commit any kind of repulsive acts. Right ever from the dawn of human society he sleeps with woman.'

'Ha...ha...ha...That's natural,' Kenchayya broke to display his common sense. In fact, he burst out briskly to weigh down the other's pool of practical knowledge.

'But d'you know what'd be the nature of erotic relationship between man and woman?'

'Of course, husband and wife.'

'But in many cases,' Rayanna continued, 'man sleeps with some women that's not permitted. Or can I say, it's immoral — a wrongdoing. He sleeps with his cousins, sisters, mothers, and in some cases with daughters. Not to speak of this, he sleeps with brothers' wives and aunts.'

'Is it?' Kenchayya nodded curious. His mouth was wide and open and his sensory organs wakeful. He looked at the younger intently.

'Yes it's what I read in books. Have you not read Shahjahan, the Mogul king? He maintained his sex with Begum Saheb, his eldest daughter as European travellers say.'

'My god!' the bigger muttered hysterically.

There fell a deep silence.

'Really...D'you know how the mullas reacted against it?' Rayanna continued desperately even without his companion's reply. 'Their verdict was that it's not a sin if a man enjoyed his fruit. Never...never the religious authorities that were the wardens of morals dared to oppose the king. D'you know how the Muslims to this day still marry their cousins. Even in medieval times, as I've read it in Alberuni's *Indica*, people had a very vague idea of biological relationships.'

'What d'you mean?' Kenchayya asked. This encouraged the other to go on narrating the medieval gender wonders.

'In those days,' Rayanna started, 'when a man died young, his wife was married to his brother. In case, the dead had no brother, the widow was married to his nearest relative. This was done to shelter the woman as well as to see that the dead found his descendants. Surprising enough, the father to the newlyborn was the dead and not the one, who really fathered it,' Rayanna broke emotionally charged. 'Have you heard anything about polyandry?'

'I think, I've not, save the story of Pandava brothers. If you don't mind tell me the tales of ancient times,' the old man still passionate asked his companion eagerly.

'Polyandry means a woman marrying many either out of love or necessity. In Draupadi's case, as it's known, she married Pandavas, the five brothers. But in other cases, usually a woman marries only two. Still to this day polyandry is practised in part of Kashmir. There mostly the poor follow it. Two or three go for a single wife. Be it known to you that only the poor people and only brothers live with a woman together. As I've read the travel accounts of Bernier, this contributes towards the reduction of population, doesn't it?' Rayanna told some history gracefully.

As Kenchayya listened more to the strange tales he turned curious to know more and more. Even a fly that sat on his Dravidian nose did not distract his attention.

'The people of Nayar community practise polyandry. And they've a matriarchal society.'

"O! Matriarchy..." the other exclaimed.

'Matriarchy means woman's dominance in human society against man's. In that kind of system, mother is supreme. She's everything that goes with the use of power. In such families, every husband is like our woman — a subordinate if not a slave,' the younger added laughing.

'How can a man live a slave to woman?'

'Why...? He can...It's possible in Nayar society. A Nayar woman's marriage is just a token marriage. A Nayar woman remains in a subordinate situation. He can't question his companion for any of her misdeeds. Nor can he oppose her illicit affairs? Really... even he can't have any considerable sway in her decision-making policies. — Though it's disgusting,' said he.

'You mean polyandrous woman rules her husband?' clearing his throat Kenchayya cried for confirmation.

'Yes.'

'So like our wives, are their husbands, aren't they?' Kenchayya said.

'Yes. If you exercise your imagination, you can easily understand the libidinous nature of such women who are the mistresses of their households. Theirs, sir, is just a token marriage. Likewise a Nayar woman marries only a Nayar man. This helps them to continue the tradition.'

'But it's all a token marriage?' the oldster broke. There was some uneasiness in Kenchayya's face as if he was afraid of being born in Nayar community next time.

'Yes, it's and Nayar woman need not spend her honeymoon with the man she marries.'

This looked astonishing.

'Wonderful! Wonderful!' the other burst cheerfully.

'She may spend it with anyone whom she loves best. Later she can live with any one also,' Rayanna continued. 'Though often she doesn't go out of her house, she's at liberty to entertain her beloved. In that case, nobody in the family questions her. Even her mother supports her,' told he with alacrity.

'Very horrible, very horrible,' Kenchayya burst into a fit of dismay.

'No, it's practised there — unsparingly,' Rayanna spoke casually. A normal tone.

'However, our's is a better society than their's, isn't it?' shot the other.

'You say. But they think their's is a superior society.'

The argument continued. Meanwhile, Kenchayya's mistress called her husband for supper. But the latter was not yet prepared to go in. He was more interested in hearing these tales. So went on it for a span of hour. Then unable to resist, Padmini herself came down.

'O!...What's this all?' she asked the men sitting there decidedly.

'No madam, it's not a dispute. We're arguing on the issue of sex and man-woman relations' said the younger blushing.

'O!...Is it?' the dame laughed. She caught the lively points. Nothing seemed to her more interesting than supporting Rayanna who apparently argued in favour of womenfolk. After all, she was a woman — to support. Then all, after arguments and counterarguments, came to a conclusion. They thought man's mode of life depends upon his tradition. Their discussion still continued in spite of Kenchayya's distaste. The latter helplessly gave up to them. Despite this, his curiosity persisted. Additional was Padmini's desire to know tales of flesh. Though it was nine o' clock, the couple did not mind listening to old events.

Encouraged by this, Rayanna persisted. He drank a glass of water to refresh his husky throat and ate betel nuts with them.

'Marriage systems,' Rayanna burst, 'are different in different countries. Social conditions contribute much towards this. For evidence, men population in Kerala is below the women's. Therefore with no hindrance, polyandry is practised there. Don't think that we human beings alone follow this. I know Brahma slept with his daughter.'

'That's wrong,' Padmini said.

'I too have heard this,' Kenchayya verified the case.

'Strange were marriage practices in olden days. You know then emperors were the gods of the earth. They did whatever they could. For evidence, the Delhi Sultans and Mogul kings lived according to their fancies. So did others. But their acts were wholly objectionable,' said Rayanna killing a masquito that bit him upon his nose.

'Was it unreasonable always?' Padmini asked.

'It's' The kings, you know, didn't act reasonably in matters related to women. They acted whimsically. If they minded, they possessed as many maids as they desired. They had been Krishnas. Besides queens, they had a large harem — even many Miss Universes. Neither the parents nor the maulvis could object it — if not queens. Only it was Nurmahal who dominated Jahangir most of the time for herself. Once it so happened that Shahjahan asked his provincial navabs to send their wives to the court once every month. But the navabs were not to go there. This was done under the pretext of enquiring their welfare. During this the king chose the exquisite women. Aware of this, Shaisthkhan, the king's uncle lived at a distant province. He was the Governor of a province in Bihar. His wife was a beauty queen. However, the men who wanted to take revenge upon him and the befallen ladies asked the king as to why he had spared her. Really pumped by this, the king asked Shaisthkhan to join a piece of army in Orissa for a battle. Meanwhile, the king's sister brought Shaisthkhan's golden deer to Delhi and the king even in the presence of his sister exploded into her. But the frustrated navab did not accept his wife and the latter committed suicide.

'Did it really happen?' Padmini asked Rayanna.

He nodded her. To quench their curiosity, he went on narrating them incidents he had read from travelogues.

'I wonder whether such things happened?' Padmini turned dubious.

'Why not? You're a Doubting Thomas…!' her husband made a countermove.

'Such events really take place,' Rayanna replied the two smiling upon them.

'Certainly?'

'See sister, the ancient kings even didn't hesitate to get foreign ladies — a dealing. A medieval Javan king had made a rule that the foreign ambassadors should bring him minimum a beautiful lady, one or two handsome men and if possible other objects as gifts.'

'O!…Did he wish the man marry the lady he got brought?' asked Padmini devoid of common sense.

'Devi, you've no brain,' Kenchayya broke down.

All fell in a peel of laughter.

'Obviously the king wanted to enjoy the lady for himself. Then he accepted the men for the sake of his daughters. Because in those days, kings didn't allow their daughters to marry.'

'That's unfair,' Padmini burst.

'Of course. The king avoided their marriage but he got them handsome men.'

'Why shouldn't we think queens entertained such handsome men?' Kenchayya poked his nose.

'No, usually such affairs were discouraged. But who knows what happened in the House of history.'

'That's true.'

Kenchayya began recollecting more events. He told how some fathers and uncles would become lovers while sisters and aunts turned mothers. He expressed his annoyance against evil deeds. When Rayanna remained silent for a moment, Kenchayya went on illustrating events — spicy. Meanwhile, it was Padmini's turn. 'A university Professor,' she began, 'gave more marks to pretty ladies and to Christian girls.'

'The whole town knows this,' broke the outsider.

No sooner this was told than Kenchayya looked disturbed. Mostly he was thinking of the fate of Radha, his daughter who went to Pampapattan University for an MA in English. He felt English literature would corrupt the young. Mostly the theme of *Sons and Lovers* agitated him. Disgusted by this, he desired to retire home.

'D'you know how the Utopians treated marriage?' Padmini asked eagerly. Since she was not shy of such things, she enquired him to add more to the stock of her knowledge.

'In Utopia, as Sir Thomas More writes marriage matters were frankly discussed. When a boy or girl wanted to see a respective person for marriage, the other was quite nakedly shown. When outsiders objected to it, the natives said them 'showing one naked while fixing a wedding was not wrong.'

'It's wrong, however,' broke the eldest.

'These events are strange,' Padmini said smiling upon both the male figures. Her smile was so bewitching that Rayanna could not help seeing her with an eye of love for a while. The presence of an outsider stimulated her. But she was not loose. She would take precaution in that. Kenchayya's oldage had made her aspire for a young one. So she had Rayanna and none smelt it.

Shortly the chatting was to end up, while Rayanna smiled at her as much as she smiled at him when chances permitted. During this, Kenchayya sat silent gazing at the stars above.

'Greenland you know,' Rayanna began, 'It's much cold there as it occurs in the extremity of arctic. Women population is scarce there for this reason — leading to polyandry. Just the same, woman is an asset of many there. Warm things are in demand too and they are shared by all. So you can think that, like our computer sharing, there is a wife sharing system. If any guest goes there, after dinner, the leading husband offers him his dame. Don't think they're ashamed of this — but accustomed. Surely guest's indifference hurts the host.'

'Wonderful!...Wonderful!' Padmini broke while the oldest sat aghast.

Upon hearing this, fear gripped Kenchayya. Now he was more afraid of the fate of his wife at home rather than the fate of his daughter at the Campus. He did not take much time to close this talk. Soon, the happy Padmini wished a goodnight to the narrator of these tales and she moved inside. However, the other two souls were at peace, Kenchayya was strangely beset by some unknown fears.

ooo